LIVING CURSED

BOOK ONE

LIZZY RICHMOND

First paperback edition November 2022

Book design by MiblArt

Edited by Lisa Howard

ISBN 979-8-9870771-0-8 (paperback)

ISBN 979-8-9870771-3-9 (ebook)

www.lizzyrichmondsbook.com

❋ Created with Vellum

This book is dedicated to my best friend and my mom. The two people who are the main reason this book is able to be out in the world. I couldn't begin to thank you enough.

I love you!

CHAPTER 1

"I'm sorry, Maisey. I'm afraid we aren't any closer to figuring out what's happening to you. I think it's time you really consider seeing the therapist I recommended."

Another doctor. Another failed attempt to figure out why my red hair was turning white, why my skin was getting paler, why even my green eyes were losing color. I knew it wasn't all in my head—I knew doctors were missing something. Every passing day, I looked more like the walking dead, and I felt like it, too. The days were only getting harder, especially with my job.

Being a waitress requires constant movement without passing out in the middle of the lunch rush or looking so weak that customers want to carry over the tray of food themselves. It's never an easy job, but when you can barely survive on your own, being a waitress is ten times harder, especially when you're too sick to get out of bed. I felt as if I were slowly watching my life fall apart and there was nothing I could do to stop it.

I was desperate and no closer to getting the answers I needed. Not from doctors, anyway…

* * *

I PULLED OPEN THE DOOR, hearing the bell at the top go off. One step inside, and I was overtaken by strong scents. One I couldn't recognize, but the other was lavender. Somebody had given me lavender one day to help me sleep because the pills weren't doing anything.

Hanging on the wall was a bright neon sign that spelled out "Let Cece See the Truth." I couldn't stop myself from rolling my eyes and fighting an instinct to run away. Far, far away.

With my arms folded across my chest, I walked across the dark hardwood floor to one of the chairs wedged against the wall. The room felt exactly the way I'd expected it to: all tack and no taste.

The crimson walls were adorned with neon lights hanging down like Christmas lights. A large dream catcher hung on each wall, and different herbs and flowers dangled from the ceiling. Shelves of crystals and rocks stood on one side of the room while skulls of all sizes were stacked on shelves on the other side. *I should not have come here,* I couldn't help thinking.

A woman walked a young man through the beaded door next to me. "You're amazing!" he told her.

"Well, the veil was open today. Let's hope for that again next week." The woman was short, with curly blonde hair that spilled onto her small shoulders. I could tell that her smile was a common fixture for her whether she meant it or not.

The young man walked out the front door with one last smile and a little skip in his step.

Cece let out a deep breath, her smile disappearing as she turned to look back at me. "Poor boy! He comes once a week to talk to his father, but the man absolutely hates his son." She tilted her head in the direction of the parking lot. "I always have to give him a pep talk. You'd think he would pick up on the fact that his father would never care about him that much."

A wave of annoyance ran through me. "I knew this was stupid," I muttered. I pushed myself up off the black chair, ready to storm away and never come back.

"I don't lie." My feet stopped at the sound of her voice. I told myself not to, but I faced her anyway. "I just tell him what he pays me to tell him. No one wants to be told they're worthless, especially not by a parent. We expect approval from our parents."

Cece stepped closer to me, a smirk instead of a smile on her face. "That's why you're here, isn't it? You wanna know about your parents. You wanna know what part of them is causing you so much pain." She turned around and walked to the beaded doorway, then swept back half of the door with one hand and looked at me. I was still frozen in place. "You've already waited twenty-one years. I think that's long enough."

Every part of me begged myself to just take off and stick with what I knew. But sticking to what I knew wasn't going to be helpful—the doctors were at a loss and I wasn't getting any better.

I took a deep breath and walked through the beaded door, stepping into much darker surroundings. The room was only dimly lit by a chandelier hanging above the central table. Smaller tables surrounded it, each one illuminated by glimmering candles. The round wooden table in the center had a glass ball sitting on it.

Cece walked around the table and sat down, ushering me

to sit. "Where would you like to start?" she asked. Her eyes were fixed firmly on mine.

My lips parted, but I didn't know what to say. I quickly shut my mouth and tried to calm the different questions running through my head. Then one thought loomed larger than the rest. "Even if you tell me things about my family, I won't know if you're telling the truth."

Cece smiled and reached her hands out towards me. Seeing as I didn't have many options, I took her hands, bracing myself to be completely let down all over again.

Cece closed her eyes. I carefully noted her expression, trying to find any sign of deception. "You were left in an alley between a gym and a coffee shop." My stomach suddenly dropped and Cece opened her eyes. "Only three buildings down from a hospital. You could have been left there with no questions asked. Must be hard to accept being abandoned in an alley instead. I bet every day of your life you've wondered why. Why would your parents just leave you there?"

I'd gone over and over that day every chance I got, as if one day I would look at the police reports and find my way to my birth parents. *Have they looked for me like I've looked for them?*

"Yes." Cece's voice dragged me out of my nagging thoughts. "They're looking for you, too."

Panic flooded through me. I shook my head and quickly stood up. "I'm not going to fall for your lies!" I snapped, then stormed out of the smaller room. I strode across the hard-wood floor and pushed on the glass front door. There was a strong resistance, like someone was on the other side and was holding it shut...except that I could clearly see no one was there.

"Let me out!" I shouted. I whipped around to face Cece, who was standing in front of the beaded door. "Unlock the door!"

"Just wear this." Cece held out a necklace. A red crystal wrapped in silver metal dangled from a chain. "It's a healing crystal. Something tells me you'll feel a change right away."

I wanted to argue, but I wanted to leave even more, so I walked over to her and snatched the necklace out of her hands. I looked back at the door and then again at her. She didn't move—she just nodded at me as if she was signaling for me to try again.

I slowly walked back to the door and put my hands on it. I pushed forward harder than usual...and then stumbled when it readily swung open. I barely managed to catch my balance.

Embarrassment stained my cheeks red. I kept going without a backwards glance, walking towards my car. Once I'd closed my car door, I tossed the necklace into the passenger seat, started the car, and started driving down the long, dark road.

The drive was silent, calming, except for the nagging feeling stirring inside of me. It was a craving feeling. A begging feeling. I glanced over at the crystal sitting on the seat. I felt like it was calling my name.

I forced myself to focus on the road. The full moon shone high above the road, pulling me into a trance. My body tensed and I gripped the steering wheel so hard that my knuckles lost what little color they had. The trees lining both sides of the road started to bend. Instinctively, my foot slammed on the brake, jolting me in my seat. My seatbelt was the only thing that kept my head from slamming into the steering wheel.

My body shifted into autopilot as I pulled over to the side of the road. Sweat beaded on my forehead; all I could hear was the pounding of my heart. I leaned against the cold steering wheel. My fever was spiking. With my eyes closed, I turned the air vents on high.

In and out... Just breathe in and out...

It took everything I had to focus on my breathing as I prayed I wouldn't lose consciousness. All I could do was wait. Wait for my heart to slow down and my temperature to lower and to maybe regain just enough energy to make it home and not have to sleep in my car. Last time I did that, I woke up to police trying to break in because they thought I was dead. Which was better than the time before that, when the person trying to get into my car knew I wasn't dead and just thought I was easy pickings. Thank God for pepper spray!

It felt as if it only took a few seconds for me to open my eyes, but that was an illusion. I never got over it fast. I didn't even want to look at the clock; I didn't want to know how long it had taken this time.

Suddenly, I felt something resting on my lap. I looked down and saw the crystal shining up at me. What little part of me that wasn't exhausted was instantly shot through with panic. It wasn't the first time something had been out of place when I finally came to. I don't know how it happens, but it does. And that scares me more than anything else.

* * *

AFTER A BRIEF SPELL, I tied my apron back on, walking out to the main part of the diner I worked in. I reached into my pocket and grabbed my pen...and then noticed a chain rubbing on my neck. *This can't be happening! How did it get there??*

I slowly reached into the bodice of the white tank top I was wearing under my white button-up shirt and fumbled for the chain. I pulled it up until I saw the red crystal hanging on the end of it. My heart fell to the floor as I remembered leaving it in my car yesterday.

"Cute necklace!" I jumped at hearing Jenna's voice. She walked past me to put a piece of paper on the service window. Her brown hair streaked with blonde highlights was neatly pulled back, showing off her perfectly put together face. She was tall, thin, and beautiful. If she weren't such an enjoyable person to be around, I would hate her. "Where did you get it?"

Every instinct told me to lie—I didn't want her to look at me like I was crazy. "It was a gift," I quickly said, dropping the necklace back down into my shirt. *I'll get rid of it later,* I vowed. *I will make sure it's as far away from me as possible.*

Outside the diner, the sky was pitch black, with clouds blotting out any sense of the stars or the moon. I enjoyed the night shift because it was the easiest shift and the most predictable.

Like clockwork, Detective Lee Washington walked into the diner and sat down at the bar. Lee was in his late forties and dark-skinned and always wore a suit. He came into the diner every night, sat at the same spot at the bar, and ordered the same thing. As I always did, I walked over with his coffee and set it in front of him. "Hi, Lee. How's the shift going?"

He smiled at me. "It's thankfully slow."

"Thankfully slow" was right. On nights like this, I got manageable money from my tables and the stress was minimal. Plus, if I got dizzy and had to sit for a while, we weren't so busy that the other waitress would curse me to hell for leaving her to fend with the customers alone. The only downside came at the end of my shift, when I tried not to be the last one to leave. Probably all the crime shows I watch make me nervous, not to mention the idea of no one knowing I'd never made it to my car if I should collapse on the way there.

When I left that night, I carried my phone and my keys in one hand and a bag of garbage in the other. I headed for the dumpster and tossed in the bag, then dusted my hands off on my dark jeans as I turned to walk to my car.

A panicked scream cut through the late-night silence. It sounded like it had come from every direction. I looked around the parking lot, astonished not to see anybody else come running. Had no one else heard what I'd heard? Had *I* even heard it? Maybe it all was in my head. Wouldn't be the first time.

The scream came again, but this time it was calling my name. It was a woman's voice. I ran into the small woods behind the diner, trying to get closer to the voice. I didn't know why, but something told me I had to find the woman who was screaming. Whoever she was, she needed me.

Wait! What am I doing? I'm running to a voice I don't recognize! I stopped. The only sound I could hear now was the racing of my heart. But it wasn't fear. It was something… different. Enticing, maybe? The feeling you get when you finally get to do something or see someone you've been waiting for your whole life?

I shook my head. *Anticipation! That's the word. But why am I feeling anticipation?*

A sudden lightness in my hand made me look down. My phone and keys were now in the dirt by my feet. My hand that had once held them started to shake. Then the ground under me started to turn. I stumbled, tripping over what had to be the roots of a tree since the next thing I felt was my back hitting bark. I let myself fall to the ground.

The darkness was coming faster than normal. The woods around me twirled faster and faster…until all of it merged together to make a giant wall of nothing.

* * *

DARKNESS SLOWLY FADED AWAY, replaced with an aching pain that traveled throughout my body. But the more aware I became of the pain, the more aware I became of the voices surrounding me. "Look who's awake!" I heard a thickly accented man's voice that I didn't recognize, followed by multiple laughs. I put my hands firmly on the ground, feeling leaves crunch underneath my weight.

"Let me help." Another man's raspy voice hit my ears as a large hand grabbed my arm, pulling me quickly to my feet in one swift motion.

I stumbled before finding my balance. The man holding my arm held me close to him and took a harsh inhale of my hair. I flinched, trying not to gag on his smell of days-old sweat and strong liquor. I looked away from him at the other two men standing nearby. They both had dangerous smiles on their rough faces. They were tall and very thin, holding their weapons with long arms—one had a sword and the other an axe. One had long hair and the other was bald, but both of them had ears sticking out from their heads. They were much skinnier than the stench-emitting man holding my arm.

"She smells good!" he said to them. He hummed in my ear, making my stomach turn. "I wonder how you taste…"

I looked up at him, horrified by the way he towered over me. He had broad shoulders and a tight grip. Something in his eyes was off—the pupils in his eyes were huge. So huge that he seemed to be looking through me.

All the disgust building up in me turned into panic. With one strong motion, I punched straight up, hitting him in the face. The sound of a hard *crunch!* hit my ears.

The man stumbled back, covering his nose with the hand that had once held me. He didn't gasp in pain—instead, he laughed a laugh that sent chills down my back.

Blood dripped down his now-crooked nose. He spat blood onto the ground, barely missing my feet. I didn't think he'd intended to miss. His large smile showed off his yellowed, crooked teeth. "This is going to be fun!"

Fear shot down my spine. My feet backed up, preparing to take off...and then I heard a howl. It was close by. The howl didn't worry me so much—I'd rather have been mauled than have those men touch me—but the look on their faces put me on high alert.

The man with the broken nose pulled out a knife. It was covered with stains I didn't even want to try to recognize. "I know you're there!" he half-shouted, half-growled. "Come out, you bastard!"

A sharp hiss cut through the air a second before an arrow went through his eye. The large man fell to his knees, gasping. He let out a high-pitched scream of agony. Then another arrow sprouted in the center of his forehead, and I knew he was dead. His body hit the ground with a heavy thud.

I glanced at the other two men, seeing that they looked as scared as I felt. Then I quickly turned around to see a tall muscular man walking out from behind the trees. He wore long, light brown pants, tall black boots, and a black shirt that was slightly ripped at the top. His skin was an almond tan and he wore his black hair tied back in a bun. He held a bow in one hand and had a quiver of arrows strapped to his back and a bag strapped over his chest. Several knives were holstered on his hip. But the scariest thing was the giant gray wolf by his side. It snarled and showed its teeth, staring at the men with icy blue eyes.

"Anyone else?" the man asked. His voice held the same accent as the other men's had had.

Without a sound, the others scattered like cockroaches back into the woods, leaving their dead friend for the animals.

"Are you all right?" the man asked me.

"I'm fine, thanks." I said, watching him carefully. I had little chance of getting away before, but I had none now, not with this man and his wolf. If he had something planned that I wasn't going to like, I was screwed.

As he neared me, I quickly took a step back. He halted at my reaction. Then his hand reached up and I saw that he was holding a white cloth. "You're bleeding," he said calmly.

I finally realized how much pain was coming from both my back and my head. I lightly touched my forehead right above my left eye, feeling a sting that made me wince.

"I just want to help," he said in the same gentle tone. This time, when he stepped closer to me, I didn't back away—instead, I let him press the cloth onto my forehead. Something cold numbed the cut. *Why did I let him get so close to me?* I wondered in the back of my mind.

Now I realized how big he actually was—easily over six feet tall, with broad shoulders. He carried himself differently than the other big man had, though. This one walked with his spine straighter, and there was more confidence in the way he moved. His arms were covered in tattoos that went from his wrists all the way up to the short sleeves of his shirt.

He pulled the cloth away and put it back into the bag, taking a step back. His eyes scanned me. Not in a way that seemed threatening, but the intensity of his gaze was a bit frightening nonetheless.

"Why are you looking at me like that?" I asked, crossing my arms over my chest.

"You aren't really dressed for the forest, especially not this one," he pointed out.

I sighed. "Well, I didn't count on going on a hike." I looked around for any sign of where I was, but I saw nothing but tall, darker-than-normal trees and a very gray sky. Then I noticed the wolf sitting next to him. It wasn't acting aggressive, but then again, it's not like a wolf has to look aggressive before it pounces. And it was staring at me very intently. "You have a pet wolf?" I asked the man.

"His name is Axel and he's not a pet," he said matter-of-factly. He let out a deep breath and carefully surveyed our surroundings. "I can get you out of the forest…"

I could hear the hesitation in his voice. "What's wrong?"

He turned around to start walking back up the hill before answering. "This is the dark forest. It's no place for…" he trailed off again.

I quickly followed him. "For what?" I asked, making him stop and look at me.

"A damsel in distress."

A wave of anger flooded over me. "I am not a damsel in distress!" I yelled. He just looked away. "And seeing as how I punched someone five minutes ago, I would be careful what you say to me!"

"Or what? You'll lie on the ground again?"

I held my breath, fighting the desire to light him up with my preferred curse words. But I didn't see that going in my favor, so instead of causing myself more trouble, I just shoved past him. "You know what? I can find my way back all on my own."

I could feel him watching me and hoped he was enjoying the view. *Such a son of a—*

A click just under my foot made me freeze.

"Damn it!" I heard the man curse. He quickly rushed to my side and bent down on one knee to move some leaves out of the way. He cursed even more. I felt my stomach drop.

That was when I noticed the device right under my foot. "What is that?" I breathed.

He looked up at me as he slipped the bag over his head. "Do not move!" he warned me. He reached into the bag and pulled out a blade that was much smaller than the ones on his hip.

I looked down at the device again, noticing the pointed edges around the circular trap. It reminded me of a bear trap, but instead of being metal, it was made of a dark wood. One that matched the trees around us. "Is that a bear trap?" I asked.

He didn't look up at me, but I could see the crease between his eyebrows. "No, it's a hell beast trap. The teeth slow it down." He pointed at to the tree to my right. "The spear attached to that tree stops it, and the poison soaked into the wooden teeth kills it."

My mind was racing as I frantically tried to sort through the information coming at me. "Hell beast…" My breath wobbled. "Oh my god, I *am* crazy," I whispered, making an effort not to look at him.

"Just stay absolutely still."

"You know what you're doing, right?"

He scoffed as if insulted by my questioning. "Of course! I set the trap."

He saves me one minute and then is the reason I could be dead the next. This is why I have trust issues…

I did my best not to move an inch, but the more my heart pounded, the more I wanted to jump out of my skin. So I focused on the man working under my foot. He moved with no hesitation, no uncertainty.

All I could hear between my thumping heartbeats was the strong wind. It kept sending chills up my arms. Every hair on my body was standing on end; my eyes were glued on the pointed teeth of the device. That's all I could think about: those sharp edges jumping up and latching around my ankle and bringing pain and death.

The man let out a deep breath of relief before looking up at me. "You can step away now."

I held my breath as I gingerly stepped backwards. The trap didn't move. Relief swept through me, taking away all of my other emotions. It's hard to hold on to anger and fear when you're just happy to not be harmed.

"I need to get out of this place," I stated bluntly, bending over slightly and resting my hands on my knees.

"Do they not use manners where you come from?" the man asked.

I took in the biggest deep breath I could before standing up and facing him. "Thank you," I said calmly, trying to ignore the bitter taste in my mouth.

"That must have been painful," he said in a neutral tone.

I sighed. "I'm not a horrible person, okay? Well, I don't try to be..." I looked at the trees again. *There's no way these were the woods I was in before!* "Where are we?"

"I told you. The dark forest."

I quickly shook my head. "No, that's not what I mean." I felt myself getting snippy, so I paused to take a deep breath. "Are we still in Maine?"

He looked at me, confused. "I don't know what Maine is. Is that where you were going?"

"That's where I *was*."

He just looked at me blankly, not seeming to understand what I was talking about.

A pit formed in the bottom of my stomach. "Oh my god..." I turned away from him. My hand went to my stomach as I fought the urge to throw up. "Way to go, Maisey! You screwed up again!" I muttered.

The man broke into my panicked rambling. "I will get you to your Maine," he said solemnly. "I give you my word."

I looked back at him. "Your word? I don't even know your name."

He stepped closer to me, holding out his large hand. "Kit Dawkin."

I slowly reached out and took his hand. His palm felt rough and large against my own. "Maisey Collins."

I may not have known where I was or where I was going, but there's one thing I knew for sure...

I have to get home.

CHAPTER 2

It was as if time didn't exist here. For one thing, there was no sun to keep track of the passing days —the sky just held the same gray clouds that intermittently burst into intense weather that could make anyone wish for death. Well, make *me* wish for death. Kit seemed completely unaffected. He just pulled out a beat-up cloak from his bag and gave it to me whenever it started raining. It was too big, but I wasn't going to complain, especially since I was wearing a white shirt. And aside from ourselves, amidst the eternal grayness, the only living thing we came across was crows fluttering in the trees.

I realized I had a watch strapped on my wrist. Would that still tell the time? I knocked on it experimentally. Nothing. No ticking, probably because its face was cracked. Then, suddenly, the hands started moving faster and faster.

I started smacking the face, trying to get it to stop and letting out an annoyed groan. Then I went straight into a figure. I looked up, meeting Kit's dark brown eyes. He didn't seem annoyed or irritated, but then again, I didn't know him well enough to be able to read him.

He glanced down at my watch. "That's not going to work out here."

"Why not?" I asked.

He crouched down by a nearby tree. Axel was already sitting next to it, acting like he'd been waiting for us.

Kit started rummaging through his bag. "You notice how we haven't seen the sun or moon since we've been here? That's because time doesn't move in these woods. Some people believe they occupy the veil between our kingdom and the kingdom of the dead."

"Well, isn't that colorful." I folded my arms, rubbing them with my hands. Kit stood up holding a bottle filled with green liquid. "What's that?"

"It's going to help me get us some food." Kit gave me a stern look. "You stay here."

"What if something comes at me?" I asked, cursing at myself for sounding so pathetic.

Kit started walking away. "That's what Axel is for." He didn't even give me a second glance.

So all I can do is hope he comes back. I don't even want to think about what will happen to me if he doesn't... I pulled the cloak tighter against my chest and walked over to the tree, sinking against it and then sliding down until I was sitting on the ground. The gray-lit surroundings were cold and dingy. I couldn't stop thinking about home. I'd never thought I would —*could*—miss it so much. I didn't have much, but it was mine.

My small one-bedroom apartment was on top of a bakery. The owner would bring me some of her desserts during very hard spells. Her chocolate muffins were my favorites. But there'd been a week when I couldn't even get up off the couch to use the bathroom, and that week, not even the chocolate muffins had been appealing. Still, she came by and fed me and stayed with me all night until I got better. She said after raising five boys, she could handle anything, and she always wanted to take care of a daughter.

When it came to work, I tried not to socialize too much. A couple of my coworkers didn't like me because I had to call in so much, but one liked me being gone because that gave her more hours. And then there was Jenna. We always worked nights together. I picked them up all the time to make up for the days I missed, and she picked up nights to pay for all the money she spent.

At work, Jenna would dress casually and just tie her hair back and she'd still get good tips just off her looks. But when she was out! Well, if beauty could kill, everyone that looked at her would be dead. Her hair was perfectly styled, her makeup was done to perfection, her nails were gleaming, and her clothes were the peak of fashion. She always said when she was out, she needed to have the looks to meet someone rich enough to take care of her. But at work, she said, "If I made enough to be able to love someone I met at a diner, I wouldn't have to work at one."

That still made me laugh just thinking about it. Her idea was backwards but amusing. Plus, she was the only person at work who cared about me. She covered for me and she brought me food when I was sick. She was the closest thing I had to a friend.

I started to wonder if my coworkers knew I was gone. I always tried to tell someone when I was sick, but there'd been a few times when I couldn't. They'd just assumed I couldn't make it in, and they were right. *How long before someone realizes I'm gone?* I wondered. *And what are they going to think? That I just left?*

A tear slid down my cheek. I quickly wiped it away when I heard footsteps coming towards me. I looked over and saw Axel sprawled on the ground, unmoving. If he wasn't on high alert, I didn't need to be.

Kit came out of the trees with the bottle still in his hand, although now the liquid that had been in it was half gone. In the other hand, he held a piece of raw meat a little bigger than his palm.

He walked over and handed me the meat. I looked at him, disgusted. "Why are you giving me that?"

"Do you know how to build a fire when the ground is wet?"

I didn't know how to build a fire when the ground was dry. I hesitated to take the meat.

Kit took out a white cloth, wrapped the meat in it, and handed it to me. I took it and then watched him arrange wet leaves in a pile. He took the meat back, put it on the leaves, surrounded the leaves with a circle of rocks, and piled sticks in a triangle over everything.

"I don't know much about fires, but I don't think you can make one in the middle of wet leaves," I pointed out.

He looked at me, and I could tell he was annoyed. "Because you know so much about being out here?" He stood up and grabbed his bag, swapping out the green jar with one filled with red liquid. He tipped a tiny bit of the liquid over the top of the triangle as I watched curiously.

The triangle suddenly erupted into deep red flames. I flinched back reflexively while Kit put the bottle back into his bag.

Kit watched the fire dance around and I found myself watching him. The scent of smoke filled the air; soon, the smell of meat being cooked lazily drifted towards us. He was right: I didn't know anything.

Time went on and on. Without a functional watch, I had no idea how long it took for the fire to die out, but once it was gone, I saw a chunk of perfectly brown meat resting in the ashes.

Kit grabbed the dagger attached to his hip, stabbed the

meat, and held it up. "I hope you eat meat," Kit said, looking over at me.

* * *

THE SECOND NIGHT was even worse than the first—as we were walking through that cursed forest, it started snowing. I fought a feeling of defeat when I saw Axel sit down, because I knew what that meant: we were staying put for the night. Kit shrugged off his bag and bow and arrows, carefully setting them on the ground.

"Why do we have to stop?" I asked, sounding more panicked than I meant to.

"We won't get very far if we freeze to death," Kit said bluntly. I tried to not let my teeth chatter. "It's going to take us a while to get out of the dark forest." Kit sat down underneath a nearby tree and Axel moved over to sit down closer to him.

I held myself as tightly as I could, trying to focus on anything but the snow. "Not a very original name for a forest..."

"There's a long Nevillian name for it, but 'dark forest' is the simple translation. Actually, it's more of a death forest. Look around—the sun barely makes it through the forest canopy." Kit obviously saw the uncertainty written on my face. "You're going to have to trust me," he added.

I scoffed. "I don't trust anyone."

Kit paused for a moment; I prayed he wouldn't push the idea. "Look, anything out here hunts during daytime, not at night. It likes its prey alert and it doesn't usually hunt animals. So we can rest tonight and start again in a couple of hours."

I refused to let my mind dwell on what "it" might be. "How do you know when it's daytime?"

Kit pointed at the wolf sitting next to him. "That's why Axel is here." Kit shifted against the tree, lying down so that his head rested against the dark wood. He was just as wet as I was, with his hair plastered down his sculptured cheeks. Axel scooted himself underneath Kit's hand. I couldn't believe how calm he was. Maybe he was trying to balance all of the anxiety that was coming out of me.

I started to pace back and forth and rub my hands along my arms. I *don't need to sleep, I just need to keep moving*, I told myself. *I need to stay focused.*

"Where are you from?" Kit asked.

I looked over at him, still pacing. "I told you before. Maine."

Kit just looked at me. "But where's that?"

I stopped, looking up at the gray sky hovering over us. "Something tells me it's not near here."

Kit didn't say anything else and I was over talking. *This can't be happening to me. I can think of so many more things I'd rather be doing than being stuck in the woods...*

My living room was small. With the TV on a stand by the wall, the coffee table, and the couch, only one person could easily move around the room. I also had a bookshelf in the corner that was stacked high with books, and the desk facing the window held my computer and piles of bills. If anyone else was in my living room, we'd have to move in a circular kind of dance to get around each other.

Despite its tiny size, I loved that room. It was cozy. I spent more time there than anywhere else. I'd sit on the couch with feet up on the coffee table and a bowl of pasta shells and sauce in my lap and fantasy shows playing on repeat. In the worlds I saw on the screen, I could pretend I wasn't sick and I wasn't alone in my bed at night. Best of all, there was always a sexy man to look at.

But instead of being in my nest, I was here. I was in

clothes I'd been wearing for days, I was wet and cold, and I was clinging to a cloak that was way too big for me. I was hiking through a forest that I didn't recognize with a wolf and a man I didn't know. I'd never really thought about what my life would be like, but this wasn't it.

I'd lost myself in my head by the time I finally stopped thinking and opened my eyes. Kit's were closed as he napped underneath the tree. I let out a deep breath I hadn't even realized I was holding.

Maybe I was just incredibly tired or maybe a spell was coming on more quickly than usual, but darkness suddenly swept over me. It was like being caught up in a crashing wave. I didn't have any time to prepare or yell for help—I was engulfed by fatigue and my senses fled.

* * *

I FELT two calloused fingers run across my cheek and brush my hair out of my face. "There's something very odd about you," I heard an echoing voice say. I slowly opened my eyes and saw a blur of lights and shadows. I blinked, clearing my vision, until I saw Kit kneeling in front of me.

I groaned, then pushed myself up and quickly wiped away the dirt stuck on my face. "Ew!" I tried to express my disgust quietly, but I still saw him fighting to keep from smirking as he stood up.

I didn't even want to imagine what my hair looked like. I brushed off my clothes and finger-combed any leaves out of my hair.

A growl made me freeze. I quickly looked over to see Axel scowling into the distance. I followed the wolf's gaze and saw two purple eyes staring at me. They were beautiful, glowing with the kind of gleam that crystals reflect.

Kit's voice came at me from behind. "Maisey, don't

move!" I could tell that he was trying not to alarm me or whatever was attached to those eyes.

I didn't move, but I wanted to. I wanted to walk over to it. To touch it. To find the source of those beautiful eyes.

Axel snarled again, then threw himself forward, disappearing into the darkness and heading towards the eyes. A hand grabbed mine, snapping me out of my trance. "We need to go!" Kit hissed. He started pulling me through the forest.

"What was that?" I gasped, doing my best to keep up with him.

Kit didn't answer—he just kept going, dragging me with him. All I saw was trees moving past, but he seemed to see more.

A sudden yelp hit my ear right before a strong weight knocked us both to the ground. I looked up and saw teeth. I closed my eyes, waiting for the pain of those sharp teeth sinking into my throat.

I didn't feel anything—instead, I heard a hard screeching sound. My eyes snapped open and I looked up. The large black furry beast standing over me whipped its head around, then toppled over and started thrashing around. It was the size of a bear, but it looked like a wolf and had the teeth of a lion. It looked like it could swallow me whole.

Now, though, two arrows had sprouted from its eyes. A familiar clicking sound hit my ears just before something whooshed through the air. The click had come from the trap encircling its back leg and the whoosh had been the sound of a large pointed log slamming it in its side. It twitched a few more times, then stopped moving entirely.

Kit walked over to the now-dead beast and ripped a knife out of its throat without hesitating. I hadn't seen him throw the knife, but I wasn't going to ask him if he had—I was too busy being grateful to not be dead myself.

Without a word, Kit shoved the beast onto its back and

then stabbed the knife into the top of its chest, drawing it down to the creature's stomach. I put my hand over my mouth and fought the urge to gag. I could only imagine the horrified expression I was wearing as Kit reached into the body of the beast, pulled out its heart, wrapped it in a cloth, and placed it in his bag.

"What's that for?" I managed to ask. He didn't say a word. He probably didn't even hear me—I might have only whispered. Or I might have yelled.

When he got up, Kit stumbled, unbalanced. I quickly rushed over to him. His shirt was ripped down the side, and three long, bloody slashes from the beast's claws ran down his ribs. "You—you need to sit down," I stammered. *I've never seen that much blood before in real life...*

Kit shook his head, nearly colliding with a tree as he tried to step forward. I put my hands up, stopping him. He only lightly touched me before he fell against the tree. "I have to find Axel… It's not safe to be here alone…." he gasped.

"I'll go find him." The words came out before I could even think them over.

Kit squinted at me, clearly annoyed at the idea of me trying to be helpful. "And do what? He's over half your size."

Kit slowly pushed himself off the tree and resumed walking past me. After only two steps, he lost his balance again. I was already there, feet planted, ready to hold him up. He just looked at me, staring with the eyes of someone struggling to keep focus.

"I'm stronger than I look." I said firmly, putting his arm over my shoulders. Kit nodded, giving me permission to help him keep going.

* * *

KIT DIRECTED me through the forest until we found Axel crouched on the ground, partially hidden behind a tree. He initially growled at our approach, making my feet freeze in place, but Kit made me take a step forward. Axel laid back down; I took that as a sign to keep moving.

I helped Kit sit against the tree. The wolf pushed himself up, limping over to Kit and lying back down. Blood stained his flanks, too.

I stared at the slashes on Kit's ribs, trying to think of the best way to handle them. So much blood and flesh exposed around so much dirt! It was begging for an infection to set in.

I looked up to see Kit staring at me. "Are you going to die?" I asked bluntly.

Kit leaned his head back against the tree. "No, I'll be fine." He slipped his bag off his shoulder.

"You need a doctor," I began. "A place this dangerous has to have a doctor around somewhere. I'm sure we can find one." Wishful thinking on my part, probably, but I could hope.

Kit sighed in frustration. "Maisey, either help me or shut up."

I pressed my lips together and gave him a slight nod. I would normally object very violently at being told to shut up, but since he might be dying, I let it go.

"Go in my bag and get out the rolled-up cloth, the bottle of black liquid, and the metal flask," he instructed me.

I bent over the bag and dug through it very carefully, trying to avoid going anywhere near the cloth-wrapped heart. He had so many bottles filled with different color liquids! "What am I supposed to do with all of this?" I asked.

Kit reached over for the metal flask. "That's for me." He unscrewed the cap and took a large swallow. "Now I need you to pour some of that water on my wound and then wrap it with the cloth." He tilted his head at the bottle I was holding.

I shook the black liquid. "This is *water?*"

"It's water with a small fish in it. It's—uh…a hunter's trick. It's black bec—because the fish release a chemical into the water that will help the wound heal." Kit paused, his eyelids struggling to stay open.

"After that, get out th' bag of orange berries." He paused, struggling to get the rest of the words out. "Three," he whispered. "Only three—need to swallow them…"

I hurriedly unscrewed the lid of bottle. "Just please don't die!" I begged him. His head fell forward.

I quickly put two fingers along his neck to feel his pulse. It was weak, but it was there. He was alive and I was going to fix this. I didn't have a choice.

CHAPTER 3

$\mathcal{E}$very hour, I found myself shifting aside a corner of Kit's bandage to check his wound. It took four hours before I noticed it starting to shrink in size. It was half its original size when Kit started complaining about having laid there for too long. After another two hours of complaining, he insisted that we start moving again no matter how much I protested that idea. The cut was healing, yes, but it wasn't completely healed, and he was still limping. And complaining. And bleeding.

But he wasn't listening. He didn't care about what I had to say—he was like a dog that had been stuck in the house all day and wanted to run around the yard. I just sighed and followed him through forest.

My willingness to follow him didn't mean I was calm, though. Every night, I sat next to him with my eyes wide open, listening to his breathing and waiting for us to resume moving. What amazed me the most after everything that had happened was that I didn't feel tired or dizzy. I hadn't even fainted ever since I'd face-planted in the dirt. But I didn't focus on that. I *couldn't* focus on that. Every time I'd started to hope I was feeling better, reality sank in and I got sick all over again.

Only when Kit was sleeping would I let myself truly look at him. Not at his tattoos, but at the scars they sometimes covered: the long slash that went up his right arm, the burn mark on his chest that peeked out from the top of his shirt, the scar that went down his left eyebrow. The scar around his eyebrow was the only one not covered by tattoos. It made me wonder what happened to him, but I wasn't going to ask.

After two days of cleaning and rewrapping his wound, Kit was able to pick up his pace and I could finally see rays of sunlight coming from beyond the trees. My feet started moving a little faster of their own accord; eventually, I hurried past Kit and into the light.

"We finally made it out!" I said happily, looking up at the sun. I smiled as I felt the sun warm my cold skin. I turned around to see Kit staring with a strange look. "Why are you looking at me like that?"

Kit shook his head and looked away.

"What?" I asked again.

"Your hair looks darker."

My hand instinctively went to my hair even though obviously I couldn't feel a color change. "It does?"

Kit nodded. I felt my smile get even bigger.

"Why is that making you so happy?" Kit asked.

I shrugged. "I think it's because we're finally out of the gloom!" I had no interest in explaining my struggles to him. I may have been doing everything I could to make sure he didn't die, but that didn't make us best friends.

"It's a rare feeling for you, isn't it?" Kit smirked, making me roll my eyes. He walked past me. I didn't hesitate to follow him.

* * *

We had walked through an empty field for maybe ten minutes before I saw a giant beige tent with two slightly smaller tents next to it. I heard a faint sound of coughing and very little talking.

I followed Kit to the biggest tent. He lifted the end of the door-sized flap and entered, holding it open for me to follow him.

I stepped in. My stomach dropped.

The tent was filled with four rows of cots, each row separated by a space just wide enough to allow people to walk through. And they were indeed weaving their way through the cots, carrying blankets, bandages, and bottles of different liquids.

Every cot was occupied. The people lying on them varied in age, but all were pale and bleeding—from their mouths, their eyes, their nose, their ears. My nostrils filled with a powerful smell. *Death.*

A young dark-skinned woman wearing a beige dress came over to us. Her black hair was neatly pinned back and her long boots went up to her knees.

Kit smiled at her. "I got two for you! I wish it was more, but…" He shrugged and reached into his bag, pulling out two cloth-wrapped lumps. Both were obviously hearts from the kind of beast we had faced in the forest. He must have killed the other one before he came across me. *So that's why he was in the dark forest,* I realized.

I took a step towards one of the people lying on the cots, trying my best not to let my distress show. "What's happening here?" I asked the woman.

The woman's brows furrowed as she disdainfully looked at me from head to toe. "People are sick. The dark forest is infecting more and more villages." The woman's tone was harsh—she clearly disapproved of my ignorance.

Kit broke in. "Be nice to her—she's not from around here."

The woman sighed, her face softening. "I apologize. It's just that you would be surprised by how many people underestimate these people's suffering. The dark forest keeps getting bigger, and its dark magic is polluting the soil. People don't realize that, though, so they harvest their crops and eat them as they would with any other crop. And then entire villages are wiped out before nightfall."

I froze at the mere thought. So many people were like *this*? "There's got to be someone who can help!" I said in what was probably a hopeless burst of optimism.

The woman gave a dry chuckle. "The King and Queen haven't done a thing for this kingdom ever since the princess disappeared."

"I'm going to take these hearts to Mary," Kit said. He turned and quickly walked away from us.

"He doesn't like listening to me talk about the King and Queen." The woman said bluntly. "More than anything, those parents want their child back, but Kit got stuck with a drunk who kicked him out as a child." She quickly shook her head. "I'm sorry—I shouldn't have said something so personal. Please forget I said that."

I nodded, but of course I wasn't going to forget. I'd been rejected for years, too, and hearing how Kit's parents had treated him sent a pain through my chest. "Isn't there some way you can get them to help?" I asked.

The woman sighed again. "We've all but gone to the castle and pounded on the front door." She went over to a table stockpiled with items, then grabbed armfuls of thin blankets and walked towards the cots.

I followed her, watching her put blankets at the feet of cots that didn't already have one. "Is there a chance these people will get better?" I asked.

She stopped and turned to face me. "Thanks to Kit, some will. The heart of a hell beast can be used to make a healing potion. We start with the young—it helps their bodies fight off the illness. But for the elderly, it's much harder. Their bodies aren't as strong. And we don't have enough hearts to help them, too."

Suddenly, my own heart started to ache, and not figuratively—a pain shot through me, making me quickly hold my breath. I put my hand on my chest and I noticed that it was quivering.

The woman looked at me, confused.

My sense of balance was shifting. Fear flooded through me; it was getting harder to breathe. I knew that either darkness was going to overtake me and I was going to have another spell like I usually did...or I was never going to wake up again.

* * *

VOICES FADED in and out in a way that made it hard to focus. A beam of light against my eyes made me flinch. "We did spend time in the dark forest," I heard Kit's voice say.

"You took her into the dark forest?" That voice was different—it was a stern one. I didn't recognize it.

"I didn't *take* her, I *found* her. I was just trying to get her out." Kit sounded defensive.

I finally got my eyes open. A few seconds later, the blurry figures resolved, forming actual people. I saw Kit, the woman I'd been talking to before, and another woman. She was older, with white skin and brown eyes. Her gray hair fell in short waves around her round face. She was huskier but shorter than the other woman.

When her hands touched me, they were warm. "Try not to move," she told me. She put her hands on my shoulders and tried to get me to lie back down. "You fainted."

I nodded. "I do that."

"That's what I said," Kit mumbled in protest.

I glared at him and sat up, ignoring how tense my body was.

Before I could stop her, the older woman pulled out the chain that had been hidden under my shirt. She studied the red crystal. I watched her carefully, noticing a light green flash in her eyes. "Where did you get this?" the woman asked.

I plucked it from her hands. I hadn't wanted it before, but I didn't want her to have it now. "A psychic gave it to me. She said it would help with the fainting and weakness. Clearly, it's doing a crap job."

The younger woman leaned towards Kit. "What's a psychic?" she whispered. Kit only shrugged, not taking his eyes off the older woman.

"You don't get this type of power from a future reader," the older woman said, ignoring them both. "There's only one witch powerful enough to bind two spells in a blood crystal."

As soon as the words "blood crystal" came out of her mouth, I started to panic. "What?? What the hell is a blood crystal?" I asked as I pulled the necklace over my head.

"If Celeste brought you here, it wasn't for your own good," the younger woman blurted out. All I could focus on was the worry on her face when she said it.

The older woman shook her head, looking away from me. "Celeste is the most selfish person I have ever had the misfortune of meeting," she said crisply. She stood and looked at Kit. "You need to get her into some clothes that will help her blend in before people start talking." She didn't wait for him to acknowledge her statement before she walked away.

The younger woman scoffed. "Good chance of that!"

Kit looked at me. "Can you walk?"

I nodded and got up, then followed him out of the tent, still gripping the crystal in my hand. No matter how hard I tried, I couldn't get my mind to shut up. *Spells, blood crystal, monsters... This can't be happening to me! I'm so far from home that I don't know if I'm going to make it back. What if I never make it back?* Just the idea of actual, real magic sent chills down my entire body.

Kit's voice broke me out of my panicked thoughts. "You scare me when you're silent. I got strangely used to listening to your rambling."

I looked down at Axel walking next to me. Suddenly, my feet froze and fear paralyzed my entire body. "I'm... I...." I stammered, unable to focus with the pounding in my ears. "Why would that woman do this to me? Why would *anybody* do this to me? I just want to feel better, to be able to get out of bed in the morning! And she puts me here with magic and monsters and spells and a freaking plague!" My breath seemed to get shorter as I rubbed my hand against my chest, trying to push away the rising panic.

I couldn't read Kit's expression and desperately wished that I could. "Only one way to find out!" was all he said. He resumed walking.

"Is that supposed to make me feel better?" I asked. I forced my legs to unfreeze and followed him, Axel trotting along next to me.

* * *

BEFORE LONG, we were standing in front of a small wooden cabin, arriving just in time to escape the raindrops starting to fall on us. The grass around the cabin rose to my knees, only parted by the well-worn path leading towards the front door. I followed Kit into the cabin.

Once inside, he pushed crates out of his way as he moved deeper into the house. Axel immediately jumped up onto the large couch pushed against the wall. It was the only part of the house that wasn't strewn with papers, weapons, and/or bottles of alcohol. "Nice place you got here," I said, watching Kit throw his things onto the already cluttered table.

"I don't spend a lot of time here and I never have guests," Kit said. He disappeared briefly behind a door, then reappeared holding a long green dress.

I snorted. "Doesn't look like your style."

Kit rolled his eyes. "It's my friend's sister's dress. They stayed here for a while and she left it. Luckily for you."

He tried to hand me the dress, but I just stared at him. "I'm not wearing that," I said.

Kit sighed. "You have to. There's no way you're going to make it through this kingdom unnoticed dressed like that."

I looked down at my jeans and t-shirt and also sighed. I was covered with a mishmash of dirt and even some of Kit's blood. "At least tell me I can take a bath. If you say you're going to wash me with bucketfuls of water, I'll lose it!"

"As much as I would enjoy that, nobody's had to do that in years." Kit gestured at the door behind him with his thumb. "You can use the washroom."

I took the dress. The green fabric felt rough against my skin. Wordlessly, I walked past him and into the bathroom.

It was big enough for a tub, a toilet, and a sink, and thankfully, it was cleaner than I'd thought it would be. That made me wonder who cleaned the place when Kit wasn't home. Like the front room, the bathroom was decked out in light-colored wood, with cabinets of the same color and a sink and toilet crafted from a dark gray metal.

I turned to face the wooden tub. It looked like a large basin with two metal bands circling the outside of it. I laid the dress on the dry sink before rubbing my hand along the tub. It was smooth—I didn't feel any gaps or grooves. I wondered how that was possible with a wooden tub, then shrugged. What mattered was that I could wash.

I filled the tub before stripping off my dirty clothes piece by piece. The muscles in my body gradually started to loosen in the warm water. At least, as loose as they could get when I was so used to being naturally tense. I let myself luxuriate in the warmth for longer than I'd meant to.

Once the water had cooled noticeably, I got out, holding a thin towel around myself as I stepped in front of the mirror. It was the first time I'd been able to look at myself in days, and I didn't recognize the face looking back at me. I was used to seeing dull, pained eyes, but these eyes were vibrant! They had life to them! Life I'd been starting to believe I didn't have in me anymore.

I could see light red streaks coming back into my cheeks, too. I was still dead pale, but not "I haven't left the house in a week" pale. Not "I could play a zombie with no makeup" pale. That alone started to fill me with excitement.

I pulled myself away from the mirror and picked up the dress. It had long fitted sleeves that flared out at the wrists and a V-neck top lined with gold thread sewn along it. I slipped it on and pulled the strings in the back as tight as I could, trying to make the best out of the much-too-large dress. It fell down my shoulders and it was going to be a struggle not to step on the hem, but it was better than wearing my thoroughly stained clothing.

"We're going to stay here until the rain stops," I heard Kit say through the door.

I sighed and stepped out of the bathroom. Now I could hear the pounding of rain against the windows. "So then I didn't need to put this dress on yet," I said.

Kit turned away from the window and looked at me, his eyes traveling over my body. I was impressed they didn't stop at the exposed part of my chest. "Stop looking at me like that."

Kit slightly shook his head and looked away. "I'm not looking at you."

I could still feel his eyes on me. I glanced around and saw Axel also staring at me. "You, too?" I asked. The wolf promptly looked away, his head sinking back onto the couch.

CHAPTER 4

The moon was full, hiding behind the clouds and skittering along with the wind. The rain had lightened, but still, it didn't seem to be going anywhere anytime soon. As I watched out the window, I could see Axel running through the trees along the cabin's edge. Kit had mentioned that full moons were the only times Axel got anxious staying indoors. But Axel wasn't the only one getting anxious—Kit was pacing around the cabin like he was going to explode if he stayed inside too much longer.

"I don't understand this place," I said, breaking the silence.

Kit stopped. "What do you mean?"

"You spend time with a wolf that I'm surprised hasn't eaten you and you spend your days in a place with hell beasts that you kill with bows and arrows. You would think that someone would have invented guns already."

He just stared at me in confusion. "I don't know what a gun is, but most animals in the forest have drunk from or end up drinking from the lake believed to be blessed by a goddess. Because of that, they heal quickly. But with an arrow in them, they can't heal until it's out, which gives you a chance to either run or fight."

My confusion matched his. "So then why don't people just drink from this lake?" I didn't even try to hide my skepticism.

Kit smirked. "It allows animals to drink from it, but people are different. Some people believe you have to be pure of sin to safely drink its waters; some believe the magic is just too strong for people to handle. Either way, no person has ever drunk from it and lived." He shrugged and started rummaging through one of the cupboards.

I sighed and plopped down on the couch. Kit asked me if I wanted some food. I declined. Kit handed me a large mug anyway, joining me with a mug of his own.

I peered at it. It was some sort of brown liquid with a strong, burning smell that somehow also reminded me of berries. I was never much for drinking other than an occasional half glass of wine when I was particularly stressed. *Then again, after everything I've been through, maybe this could calm my nerves*, I mused.

I took a drink from the mug, letting it burn my throat on the way down. Instantly, I gagged and started shaking my head.

I heard Kit laugh. He'd swallowed his without even flinching. "You need better taste buds," I said. I set my mug down on the coffee table.

"You don't drink much, do you?" Kit asked. I shook my head. I watched him take another swig, finishing it, and slam his mug down on the table. He looked at my almost-full mug. "You gonna finish that?"

I shook my head. "Go ahead." I sat back on the couch, feeling a heavy weight fall over me. Kit polished off my mug, too. "You're not used to being inside, are you?"

He shook his head. "I like being outside—I feel much

more free there than when I'm stuck between walls. It's not always safe, but that's the fun part." He grinned at his glass. Whatever he was thinking about, he was enjoying it.

Then he looked back at me, still with that same smile on his face. I knew smiles like that. It was the type of smile that could charm the pants off any woman he wanted. Except for me. My pants-now-a-dress was staying on. "I have a question for you."

I nodded.

"What's wrong with you?"

"What do you mean?"

"Your hair, your eyes, and the fact that you keep fainting —I doubt you do it for fun."

I glanced down at the lock of hair falling over the front of my shoulder. "I looked more like a zombie before." I'd always hated looking at myself in the mirror. It's hard to accept how other people see you when *you* hate how you look.

"Don't do that," Kit said like he was reading my mind.

I looked up at his dark brown eyes.

"You're beautiful."

I felt my cheeks quickly heat up and hastily looked down at my lap. "Are you trying to get me into your bed?"

"Trust me, if that happens, you'll be bringing me to yours."

I peeked at him and saw him looking inside the empty mug as if he'd find a hidden hatch with more liquor. "Are you drunk?"

He looked at me with a raised brow. "Are you dodging the question?"

I sighed and lifted a shoulder. "I don't know what's wrong with me." Sadness replaced embarrassment. "Do you know what it's like to feel like you're dying and then be told it's all in your head?" My breath got shaky. I'd never actually uttered those words out loud before. I shook my head, trying to push away my feelings. "I'm really tired."

"My room is in the back. Rest. I'll be here," Kit said.

I just nodded and got up, then walked away without looking at him. I opened the door and quickly shut it behind me. *I refuse to fall apart. If I let myself break, I might not be able to put myself back together.* Tears fought to escape. *Stop it! Stop... Stop! Maisey Rose Collins, stop it right now!*

I held my hair back from my face, taking in deep breaths. Once my breathing was more regular, I started looking around the room.

The bed stood against the wall, flanked by two carved nightstands. One was stacked with books and the other with papers. Across from the bed was an intricately carved dresser and a full-length mirror. Brown curtains covered the only window in the room. The bed with its pale beige covering looked like it was never slept in, which wasn't a surprise. If Kit didn't like being inside, why would he want to sleep in a bed?

I wasted no time getting into it and pulling the thick covers up to my chin. Before long, I succumbed to darkness.

THE DARKNESS SLOWLY PULLED AWAY. I couldn't see anything around me but darkness. Rounded, smooth stones were cold against my bare feet. I wore a long red dress with a corset top that was tightly tied in the back, firmly holding up my breasts. Two straps went down my shoulders and a slit went up my right leg, all the way to the middle of my thigh. Each side of the slit was embroidered with small red crystals. My vibrant red hair was in loose curls that fell over my shoulders.

I looked up to see a bright full moon hovering over me. "Can you feel it?" someone asked. I didn't recognize the voice, but chills ran through me. "The power that's radiating through you."

My hands started to shake. I looked down to see red glowing from my fingers. But I wasn't scared or worried or angry—I felt nothing.

The voice spoke again. "You will." A powerful screech filled the air.

I quickly covered my ears, screaming and fighting the urge to fall to my knees.

* * *

A LOUD CRASH jolted me back into Kit's bedroom. I gasped for air as I felt one arm slide under my knees and another go around my shoulders. I was lifted up and carried out of the room.

Kit's voice. "Maisey, you need to listen to me." All I could do was nod. "I need to know if you have the mark."

"What...what was that noise?" I asked, trying to catch my breath. He put me down, depositing me into a chair by the table. The other chair, I saw, had shattered into pieces.

Kit lifted the sleeves of the green dress, scanning my arms. "Kit!" I nearly shouted. "What is going on?"

"Soul suckers only go after people who've been marked. I need to know if you have a mark."

What?? That didn't help my confusion at all. I opened my mouth to speak, but another threatening screech pierced my ears.

Then a memory hit my mind. "I have a birthmark," I blurted out. I bent over and lifted the hem of the dress, pulling it up to the top of my left leg. The center of my inner thigh bore an approximate circle the size of a nickel with the smudged image of a tree inside the circle. I'd always wondered why it looked like a recognizable image instead of a splotch.

Kit let out a hiss. "Death tree," he said as he knelt in front of me. He pulled his dagger from his holster. "Maisey, this is going to hurt like hell."

I quickly put my hand over my mark. "What are you doing?"

"The soul sucker isn't going to go away until I destroy the mark…which means I have to cut into it. Deeply."

The screeching got louder. I closed my eyes, tears pricking the corners of my eyelids. I slowly pulled my hand away from my leg and gripped the bottom of the chair with both hands.

"I'm sorry." Kit pressed the blade into my thigh. I pressed my lips together, fighting the scream building inside of me, unable to stop tears from flowing down my cheeks. Another screech sounded, but it was farther away.

I blinked, trying clear my vision, and watched Kit hold a cloth against my thigh. "Just breathe," he instructed. After another moment, he wrapped another strip of cloth around my thigh and tied it tightly.

I cursed at the pain, slowly unclenching my hands and then curling and uncurling them as I tried to calm my breathing. Kit got up and fetched a mug of something.

When he offered it to me, I shook my head. "I don't want any more of that nasty liquor," I said, wiping away tears.

Kit gave me a faint smile. "It's just water."

I gratefully took the mug from him and sipped. "I've had that birthmark all my life." My voice cracked. "But why?"

"I don't know." Kit leaned against the back of the only free chair left at the table.

"Why didn't that thing—whatever it was—come at me before?"

Kit sighed. "Soul suckers don't go into the dark forest, but they do like to travel in rain. They fear fire, and rain keeps them protected." Guilt fell over his face. He looked away from me, trying to hide it, but I saw it nonetheless.

"So it was…coming at me while I was sleeping?" I asked.

"Yeah. I had to break my nice chair trying to fend it off." Kit gave me a slight smile, but it was more of a bitter one than a joking one.

"Well, my thigh hurts worse than how it felt to have my soul being sucked out."

Kit nodded, then went to the couch to get his bag. He rustled through it and pulled out a small wooden box.

"What's that?"

"It's something to help with the pain, but you need to lay down on the couch." Kit walked over to me. "Can I pick you up?"

"At least you asked this time…" I half-grinned at him.

Kit hooked one arm under my knees with the other under my back, then lifted me with ease, bringing me to the couch. He perched on the coffee table and slid open the top of the box. I saw a pile of yellow leaves.

Kit picked up a single leaf. "Put it under your tongue—it will help with the pain. But I should warn you that you're going to feel out of it. It's strong."

I took the small leaf, looking at it. "A leaf with a warning label. That's new."

"You aren't going to remember anything, either."

I snorted. "You promise you aren't going to take advantage of me?"

I could see Kit fighting a smirk. "Suddenly you don't trust me?" He sobered. "I give you my word that you'll be perfectly fine."

I stared at him for only a moment before I put the leaf under my tongue. It didn't taste like anything, but a wave of pleasure slowly rose inside of me. My eyelids got heavy; I laid my head back against the arm of the couch. It felt like I was starting to float up into the air. Everything blurred around me. I'd never felt so relaxed before. "What happens if I take another one?" My voice came out tired and quiet. It didn't feel like it had actually come from my throat.

"You need to sleep," was all he said.

Darkness took over, along with a calming scent. Beautiful, fragrant flowers were dancing around me. The sun was shining on my skin. Birds were chirping in my ears. I felt like I could sing and dance forever and never feel a bad thing ever again.

* * *

I DIDN'T KNOW how long I'd been out. The only thing I did know was that I was lying on my side and staring at Kit, who was asleep in the chair across from the couch. A sense of peacefulness still suffused the air.

My fuzzy brain started thinking about the sickness, the mark, the soul sucker. All of it was my fault, but what had I done to deserve this? Maybe I hadn't done anything. *Maybe what I'm forced to suffer through is just my...fate.*

Kit must have felt me staring at him, because he suddenly startled awake. He sat up straighter. "You seem to be thinking rather hard."

I half-chuckled. "Do you think some people are born to feel pain?"

Kit took in a sharp breath. "Life isn't that simple. If it were, there wouldn't be so much to figure out."

I let out a deep breath. "I can't remember the last time life was simple."

Kit just nodded, but I could tell he could relate in more ways than he was going to say out loud.

CHAPTER 5

My entire body was throbbing. I pulled myself up, resting my elbows on my legs and holding my head in my hands. No floating delight came from that leaf anymore. I wanted another one, but I knew Kit wouldn't allow that.

I slowly got up from the couch and went outside. Kit was already standing by the front door with Axel, scanning our surroundings, his ever-present bag on his shoulder. "Are you ready to keep going?" he asked.

I nodded. He handed me a jar of water.

"Thanks," I whispered. My throat felt weak.

"It's just water." Kit pointed out. He closed the door and started walking away from the cabin.

I fell in step next to him. "I don't mean just for the water. I know you didn't want to cut into my birthmark, but also I know you had to."

He gave me a sharp nod. "I gave you my word to get you home. I always keep my word."

"Why?"

"I don't understand what you mean."

"You've gone through a lot of trouble to keep your word. Most people wouldn't waste their time."

Kit shook his head. "It was no waste."

I opened my mouth, but the words got caught in my throat. So I just pressed my lips together and walked with him in silence.

* * *

KIT STOPPED on the street outside of a multistory stone building. Voices streamed out of it. Through one of the windows, I could see a woman with no clothes on taking the red curtains down from one set of windows and putting up white ones in their place. Men were coming out of the building with large smiles on their faces as others walked in.

"What is this place?" I asked even though I already knew the answer.

"The Inn." Kit shrugged, then looked at Axel and motioned the wolf towards the woods surrounding the building. Axel took off running.

"Where's he going?" I asked.

Another shrug. "He never goes far." Kit led me to the inn's entryway. He held open the door, letting me in first.

I stepped in, followed closely by Kit. My face scrunched at the strong scents of old beer and sex. I felt like dozens of eyes were staring at me; I wanted the floor to swallow me up whole.

A hand touched my back. "Come on," Kit said. He led me to a table in an unoccupied corner. We sat down on the benches.

I watched women bring drinks to the handsy men. The men pulled the women onto their laps and dragged off their clothes, exposing them to everyone. Others were having very obvious sex in the corners of the room.

A woman with her black hair in a braid made her way over to our table and set down two wooden mugs and a pitcher. Her prominent breasts were edging out of her tight black dress. "Hello, handsome," the woman greeted Kit. She winked at him and then smiled at me. "I see you brought a friend."

"I'm just having a drink this time." Kit smiled back at her. I couldn't stop my from eyes rolling. I looked away from them and focused on the women who were accompanying men up the stairs. Kit was obviously a regular. The existence of the inn didn't bother me, nor did what was happening at some of the tables, but I couldn't stop imagining what Kit did here.

"And I'm looking for a favor." Kit's voice made me snap my attention back to him.

The woman nodded and looked at me again, scanning me like I was a piece of meat. I was sure she was used to feeling that way, too. "Come with me, sweetie."

I looked at Kit, unsure, but he just nodded and filled one of the mugs. I sighed and stood up, then followed her up the stairs.

"The name's Alice," she told me when we got to the top. She led me past closed doors with fake moans coming through them.

"Maisey."

Alice went to a door at the very end of the hall, then opened it to let me inside. "I'm just supposed to give you a change of clothes."

I hesitated, looking down at the dress. I realized that somehow it had gotten even bigger than it had been the first time I'd put it on. I nodded and stepped into the room.

Alice shut the door behind us, then took the key off the hook next to the door and locked it. "No one comes in here but the girls," Alice explained. "And as far as the curtains go, white means open, red means taken, and black means off-limits." She walked over to the dresses hanging in a corner.

"Why are you doing this?" I asked her.

"My job or the favor?"

I shrugged. "Both?"

Alice picked up a red dress. "My mother was a whore. After she died, I thought I could be like a normal woman— take care of kids and a husband. I was even in love! Or at least, I thought I was. Until he reminded me who I was and who I was meant to be." Alice sighed and handed the dress to me. "A whore is a whore is a whore."

I held up the dress. It would be long enough to cover my legs, but the sleeves were short and bulky at the shoulders. I quickly slid out of the green dress and into the red one. Although it was still loose, it was a better fit. Definitely an improvement.

"As for the favor?" Alice grabbed a black corset. "Kit saved my stupid brother when he went into the dark forest. I owe Kit my life. Or my brother's life, I should say. Turn."

I turned around, letting Alice wrap the corset around me and then lace it up. It was stiff and had embroidered red flowers on the fabric. "This will be tight, but it's easier to move in than anything else I've got," she told me. "And with Kit, you're going to need to be able to move."

I tried to stop myself from imagining what they'd done together. Still, I couldn't stop myself from asking, "You've known him a long time?"

Alice chuckled and tightened the strings. "Long enough. I know his brother better, if that's what you're asking."

I shook my head. "I wasn't asking that."

Alice scoffed. "When you've been in a place like this for as long as I have, you can see love coming from a mile away."

I felt every wall I had go up in an instant. "You have no

idea what you're talking about!" I felt an awkward laugh leave my body.

Alice finished lacing the corset and stepped back. I turned and looked at her. "He's just helping me get home."

Alice just nodded, looking down at the white sneakers I was wearing. With the oversized the green dress, no one could see them, but the hemline of this new red dress was shorter.

Alice shook her head. "Take those off."

I sighed and sat down on a nearby bench. Alice handed me a pair of black leather Grecian-looking shoes that had lacing meant to be wrapped around the legs and tied at the knees. I awkwardly managed to fasten them in place with Alice's help and then stood up.

Alice smiled at me. I had to admit, from the dress to shoes, now I looked like I actually belonged here.

She took me back down the stairs and to the table where Kit was finishing his drink. I felt like everyone at the bar was staring at me. So was Kit, I saw when I sat back down at the table. I frowned at him and kicked his leg.

That didn't seem to faze him, but he did look away from me as a blonde woman with large breasts walked past us. "I'll be back. Stay here." Kit got up and followed the woman towards the stairs.

I wanted to say, "Yeah, when you're done with her," but I kept quiet and did my best to hide my irritation.

I could feel jealousy raging inside of me. The idea of staying at the table while Kit was doing whatever he wanted with whomever he wanted was too much. I stood up and walked towards the door.

A man quickly blocked my path, making me stop before I crashed into him. He had a drunk grin plastered on his face. I didn't want to go anywhere near him or his hardness in his pants.

"You look new. Why don't I break you in?" He took my arm, getting inches from my face. "I promise to be gentle."

I tilted my head away in disgust and caught sight of a glass bottle next to us on the bar. All I could feel was my heart pounding in my chest. Everything in my sight turned red as I grasped the neck of the bottle, swung it over his head, and watched him fall to the ground. It was as if I were watching myself from outside my body.

Another man shouted and rushed towards me. I swiftly kicked him in the groin with all my might. He dropped to his knees. I slammed my knee into his face.

A third man pushed himself up from his chair, shoving aside the woman who'd been on his lap. But before he could take a step, a silver blade slid in front of his neck and made him freeze. Kit stood at the end of that dagger. "Don't worry, we're on our way out," he said calmly as he motioned for me to walk out the door.

I stumbled out, rubbing my eyes. Kit grabbed my arm and started pulling me down the dirt road. "Are you just trying to cause more problems?" he snapped.

I quickly pulled my arm out of his gasp. "I'm sorry! Maybe I should have followed your lead and let him take me upstairs!"

Kit scoffed, shaking his head. I noticed him smiling as he walked away from me. My rage deepened, sinking into the depths of my being.

I hastily caught up to him. "What's so funny?" I asked through my teeth.

Kit snorted. "I'm glad to know that jealousy travels through realms."

"I am not jealous!" I huffed. Axel slid out from behind a tree and joined us.

"Then why are you so bothered?" Kit asked.

I stopped. It took all of my self-control to not to explode

in curses. I let out a deep breath. "I am just trying to get home and *not* be stuck with perverts while you get your rocks off!" I yelled. It was the tamest of what I wanted to say.

Kit paused. He had that amused smirk on his face again. "Her name is Julianne. She helps Alice run the inn. She used to be a whore, but she's not anymore. She knows everything from flowers to magic, and not just in this world, but in others, too. I figured if anyone would know about Maine, it would be her. The only reason I brought you here is because I couldn't leave you alone at my house, plus I would have wasted time going back to get you…and you're the one who's in a hurry to get out of here."

He folded his arms and looked at me calmly. "Now, do you have any more problems you need to blame me for?"

Guilt flooded me and my cheeks reddened. "Well, aren't you full of good ideas!" I resumed walking.

He did, too. "Why do brush me off when I'm just trying to help you?"

I made myself look at him. "I'm sorry, okay? I have a habit of shutting down. It's not personal."

Silence fell between us. An unbearable silence. I wish I could tell what he was thinking.

"That was hard for you, wasn't it?" Kit finally asked.

"I think I threw up a little in my mouth," I admitted.

Kit chuckled, then sobered. "I get it—my mother died when I was just a boy and my father found himself deep in a bottle. I spent most of my nights alone and outside in the cold. That's where I met Axel." Kit smiled down at the wolf trotting along next to him. "I wasn't the only one fighting for life outside." He shrugged. "Outside was always better than the rage waiting for me inside."

I felt my tension draining away. "Alice said you have a brother."

"We don't talk much," was all he said to that.

I braced myself. "My parents left me in an alley all alone when I was a few months old," I said quietly. "I bounced from house to house with people who would smile at me as they lied. Tell me I could trust them as they stabbed me in the back. Kind of makes it hard to trust someone."

Kit shook his head. "Assholes."

I chuckled. "Yeah, assholes."

* * *

IT WASN'T long before I heard someone call out for Kit. He stopped, smiling. I followed his gaze and saw a dark-skinned man walking towards us. He was taller than me but not as tall as Kit, slim but with muscles showing in his arms. Black curls covered his head. Just like Kit, tattoos covered his arms, tracing their way down from his shoulders left bare by his sleeveless gray shirt.

He looked at me with a charming smile. "What are you doing with such a beautiful woman?"

"Leave her alone!" Kit playfully smacked his friend's chest, making him laugh. "Maisey, this is Jasper." Kit motioned from Jasper to me. "Jasper, Maisey."

Jasper held out his hand. I took it. "It's very nice to meet you." He pressed his lips softly against the back of my hand.

"You, too." I smiled at him as he released my hand.

"Where are you two off to?" Jasper asked Kit.

"Believe it or not, we were coming to see you."

Jasper nodded. "Well, let's go, then!" He started walking with us. Just by the way Kit seemed to relax with Jasper around, I could tell they were good friends. I relaxed a little, too.

CHAPTER 6

I followed Jasper and Kit down the road. We turned down an isolated path and then headed up a large hill. I knew the two men were talking about me—I heard Jasper ask Kit why he was traveling with a whore and Kit tell him I wasn't one. "You only spend time with whores," I heard Jasper reply.

After that, I stopped listening. There was nothing more I wanted to hear.

We came to a small house at the top of the hill that was surrounded by woods. It looked much like Kit's cabin, but unlike his, the grass around this one was perfectly trimmed.

Jasper was the first to reach the front door. He flashed a cocky smile at us. "Welcome to my home!"

But before Jasper could open the door, it flung open, making him stumble. Standing in the doorway was a woman who matched Jasper in looks, although she was shorter and wore her long black hair pulled back in a braid. It was tied off with a green bow that matched her tight-fitting green dress. "What are you doing?" She sounded unamused.

"Trying to let our guests in," Jasper said, glaring at her.

She looked at me with a small smile. "I'm Beatrice."

"My sister," Jasper quickly added.

"I'm Maisey," I said in greeting.

Beatrice waved a hand at us. "Come in!"

The front of the cabin was occupied by a living room and a kitchen. A small table stood in the center of the room. I moved around it, making my way to the couch.

Kit walked in last, shutting the door behind him. "Good to see you, Beatrice," he said. She smiled and lightly touched his arm before walking into the kitchen.

Kit set his bow and arrows down by the door. I could tell that being here was second nature for him. This cabin was smaller than his, but it was cleaner and smelled faintly of flowers and cinnamon.

"Kit, why don't you help me outside?" Jasper asked. He didn't wait for Kit's nod before he walked back outside.

I waited for the door to shut behind them before I joined Beatrice in the kitchen. "How long have they been friends?" I asked.

She chuckled. "For as long as I can remember. Both Kit's older brother and ours were in the Giant Ogre war together."

I felt my eyes widen. "The Giant Ogre war?"

Beatrice nodded. "Yeah, you know, the war that lasted seven years."

"I'm not from around here."

She gave a quick nod. "Of course not." She looked like she was going to say something else, but she pressed her lips together instead. After a beat, she looked back at me. "Giants and ogres were fighting over territory across the sea. Ogres were getting slaughtered, so the King sent soldiers to help them."

"Help the ogres? I thought they were flesh-eating monsters."

Beatrice smiled. "They used to be. But like everyone else,

they evolved. They started living under the rule of the giants. They didn't believe in war—they grew their own food and were basically self-sufficient. But their king hated it. He even banned marriage between ogres and giants! If they ever had a child together, all of them—the child and the parents—were to be killed on sight. Then came an uprising and down came the tyrant. It's a miracle that hasn't happened here yet given how upset people are with our King and Queen." Beatrice sighed and put a hand on her necklace. I hadn't noticed it before.

The front door swung open and Jasper stepped inside. "Well, ladies, Kit and I are leaving," he called out.

We both turned. "What?" I asked.

"We're going on a little trip." I stared at him, waiting for him to say he was joking. "Don't worry! We'll be back."

I headed straight for the door and pushed past Jasper, bursting outside. Kit was standing a few feet from the door, staring up at the sky.

"Jasper says you're leaving!" I shouted.

"Yes. And you're going to stay here with Beatrice," Kit stated matter-of-factly.

"Why? Where are you going?" I asked, not lowering my voice.

"I need to find some answers. And you'll be safe here."

"I don't want to stay here while you go looking for answers without me! Why can't I just go with you?"

Kit let out a deep breath as he stared at me. "I've gotten you this far. Just trust me to handle the rest of it."

I crossed my arms. "Fine. All right. I'll stay." My eyes fell to the ground in defeat.

Kit stepped closer to me. His warm, rough hand lightly touched my cheek. I lifted my head and looked into his dark eyes, holding my breath. His eyes were so dark they were almost black. Behind them was a storm. *He's hiding something.* I couldn't see much in his face, but I could see that.

"I gave you my word that I will get you back home. Now I need you to give me yours. Jasper always protects his sister. While we're gone, I need *you* to protect her."

I couldn't stop myself from scoffing. "You trust *me* to protect someone in a world where Hell Beasts exist?"

Kit chuckled and lowered his hand. "I think you're stronger than you look."

I nodded. "I'll try my best. I give you my word."

Kit smiled at me. I didn't trust myself to say anything else —I just turned around and went back into the house, passing Jasper on my way.

I wasn't scared about being left behind, nor did I think that Kit wasn't going to come back. What put a knot in my stomach was wondering what Kit might be hiding. *What is he looking for? What is he going to find?*

A voice broke into my thoughts. "Worried?" I looked up. I hadn't even realized I was pacing back and forth in the small kitchen, staring at the floor and biting my nails.

"Maybe I should make you some tea." Beatrice made a shooing motion, waving me towards the couch in the living room.

I obediently sat and waited. After a few minutes, Beatrice walked over to me with a teapot in one hand and two empty mugs in the other. She set them down on the small coffee table.

Her necklace was dangling freely on her chest, finally giving me a good look at it. It was a small pink crystal hanging from a gold chain. "How long have you been with Kit?" she asked. "He doesn't usually take women with him when he leaves the inn." Her tone was straightforward, with no shade of judgment.

"I'm not..." I struggled to think of the right word to use,

especially since the word "inn" seemed to mean something different for me than for everyone else. "I don't work there!"

Her eyes scanning my outfit. I could tell she didn't necessarily believe me.

"I got the clothes from a woman at the inn—I don't have any of my own," I explained. *Except for my favorite pair of jeans that Kit tells me I can't wear...*

Beatrice walked out of the room without saying a word, then came back holding a light purple dress. "If you go around in a dress like that, people are going to think you're from the Inn. And that isn't going to end well," she said. She offered me the dress. "It might be a little tight around the chest, but it should still fit."

I stood up and took it from her gratefully. "Thank you." I watched her wrap her hand around the pink crystal again. "Why do you do that?"

Beatrice quickly dropped the crystal under her dress. "Do what?"

"Play with the crystal when you talk to me."

Beatrice took a deep breath and I thought about taking my question back. "It's not because of you," she finally answered. "It's… It's to keep my mind from…wandering. In a way the Gods wouldn't approve of."

I stared at her for a moment, confused, before I realized what she was trying to tell me. It wasn't just me she was thinking about—it was women in general.

Beatrice looked down at the teapot. "You probably think less of me."

"Not at all! I'm just still a little confused."

Beatrice poured tea into our mugs. "The priest in the city says you must wear the crystal of the God you are offending in order to focus on making things right. And on following their path. My brother may be understanding, but most people aren't."

Screw 'em! I thought.

"What?"

Oops! Maybe I hadn't only thought that… "People are going to have a problem whether you live the way they want you to or not, so you might as well be happy," I shrugged. "The only person who has to live with your mistakes—with your regrets—is you. But for what it's worth, you have my support either way."

Beatrice chuckled. "You aren't from around here, are you?"

"No. And from what Kit says, I guess my home is very far away." I smiled at her. "I'm gonna change." I walked into the bedroom Beatrice had emerged from with the dress.

The room was full of colors and flowers—red, orange, and yellow flowers twined along a vine around the single bedroom window, and the nightstands framing the bed each had a vase atop them that were filled with purple, green, and blue flowers. The bedsheet and pillows were embroidered with cascades of pink flowers.

I pulled at the strings behind my back, freeing myself from the corset. It took a few minutes of awkward tugging before it and the dress fell to the ground. I picked up the purple dress and slid it over my head. It was softer than the green one and smelled like lilacs. It flowed down my body and stopped just above my ankles, showing off the shoes I'd gotten from the inn.

Suddenly, I heard a loud crash that made the hair on my arms stand up. "Beatrice!" I called out.

I didn't get an answer. I was about to open the door when it swung inwards.

An older man walked into the room, his stony face lined with wrinkles. It wasn't his blue eyes or sandy brown hair that caught my attention, though—the daggers on each side of his waist were what made my stomach twist.

He shut the door, and I quickly took a step back. "What the hell are you doing?" I asked, trying to hide my fear. "And who are you?"

He stepped closer to me, his features betraying no emotions. "Aren't you a pretty one?"

"Get away from me!" I demanded.

In response, he sat down on the bed. "Don't worry—I'm not going to touch you." He rested his hands on his thighs almost sedately.

"Who are you?" I repeated.

He just stared out the window, seemingly uninterested in me. "Jasper is behind on his payments, and we're here to collect." He reached over to his right hip and drew the dagger from its scabbard. It was a slim, silver-plated blade with strands of red and gold metal twisting down the length of the black hilt.

He looked up at me, his expression finally displaying a hint of curiosity. "Whose dagger is this? Your friend pulled it out and tried to use it against me. It is a remarkable blade."

I felt my eyes narrow. "Where is she?"

"Making a payment."

I rushed towards the door, but the man quickly grabbed my arm, stopping me. "Let go of me!" I shouted. I tried to push him away. He almost lost his grip before he grabbed my other arm.

"You stupid girl!" he nearly shouted, his face only inches from mine.

I pulled away hard, trying to free my hands; he pulled me back towards him, making me slip. He took advantage of my stumbling to spin me so that we both fell onto the bed.

He pinned me firmly in place. "Listen to me!" he hissed. "If you go out there, he'll take you, too. It's her or you!"

My heart was pounding so hard that I could feel it throbbing in my ears. "Get off me!" I gasped again. My skin felt like it was on fire.

Somehow, I pushed hard enough to force him away from me, hard enough to slam him into the wall. I felt like I was going to suffocate. Cold metal touched my hand as the room around me started to change.

I was no longer surrounded by flowers. Things were crashing down around the room. I felt panic course through me in a wave, knocking me to the ground, too. Screams came from under me. They weren't mine. They started whirling around me in a storm, sending sharp pains through my body.

"MAISEY!"

Silence suddenly descended, taking away my panic and pain. I was no longer standing in the bedroom—I was standing over the body of a man, and I was still gripping the red-and-gold dagger that I had apparently plunged into his chest.

My hand shook as I let go of the dagger and slowly straightened up, my stomach turning at the sight of so much blood gushing from his stomach and chest. The floor was slowly becoming a deep crimson pool.

"Maisey!" Beatrice's voice snapped me out of my shock. I shook my head hard and then rushed mindlessly out of the room. I kept running through the house, bursting through the front door and into the grass. My stomach clenched and my body arched over, tense and rigid as I unloaded all my fear, shock, and disgust. Tears stained my cheeks as my muscles spasmed.

Finally, the gagging and pain subsided. I was still gasping, but at least I could consciously breathe again. I looked up to see Axel sitting next to me, watching me. His long nose was covered in blood.

"What the hell happened to you?" I asked. Axel just looked

behind him at the woods. I didn't know what he was looking at, but something told me I didn't *want* to know.

My knees buckled and I pitched forward. I concentrated on stopping my muscles from spasming again as more waves of disgust rippled through me.

I don't know how long I sat there with Axel watching over me. Eventually the wolf shifted, looking past my shoulder. I forced myself to turn my aching body to see what he was looking at.

Kit was striding over to me. "We need to get you out of here," he said when he reached me. He quickly threw a cloak over me, then fastened it at the neck and drew up the hood.

"I don't—I don't know what happened," I stammered. "He —he said Jasper didn't pay his debt. He said Beatrice had to pay for it. I was just trying to protect her…"

Kit rested his hands on my shoulders. "Listen, Jasper is going to get someone to clean up the bodies, but people are going to be talking about what happened. You can't be here."

I nodded. Kit slipped his hands from my shoulders and extended them to help me up, then led me down the back of the hill into the woods.

"Where are we going?" I asked once the house was out of sight and there was nothing but trees.

"We're going to get answers."

CHAPTER 7

The woods grew denser and thicker, but we kept walking. I kept asking Kit questions about Jasper's supposed debts; he kept asking me what had happened to the men who had died. I didn't have an answer, so he didn't give me an answer, either.

Finally, we stepped out of the woods and into a cluster of little houses. Kids ran around outside, their laughter filling the air. Some people were walking around with baskets of clothes, some had baskets of food, and some were hanging clothes on lines to dry.

We walked through the village to a lonely house at the back. I felt like I was being watched, but when I looked around, I didn't see anyone—every person I'd seen when we'd first emerged from the woods had rushed into their homes and shut their doors and windows.

"Apparently, no one wants to know how this is going to go," I said.

Kit sighed. "Celeste is a liar—under no circumstances can we trust her. But if she brought you here, then there has to be a reason for it."

"What makes you think she'll tell us that reason?"

"I don't know if she will, but maybe we can convince her that telling us would be in her best interest." Kit lifted his hand to knock on the dark wooden door. He looked at me. "Just let me handle this."

"Fine," I said immediately. *I just want answers.*

Kit knocked once. The door opened.

I assumed that the woman standing there was Celeste. Her long black dress looked like a tent on her small frame. Its short sleeves only covered her shoulders, but she wore layers of blue, green, orange, and red crystals around her neck that were only partially covered by her curly blonde hair. Her eyes were a pale white. Their striking color—or lack of it—made it hard to look her in the eyes, but that didn't stop me from glaring at her as memories of a bright neon sign that said "Let Cece See the Truth" flashed through my mind.

My eyes narrowed. "Cece!" I hissed.

Celeste just smiled, ushering us forward. "Welcome, Maisey. Come in."

Her smile enraged me. "*You* did this to me! *You* brought me here with that damned crystal you gave me!"

I lurched forward, ready to pound her face in, wanting to kick her or punch her or even throttle her, but Kit wrapped a burly arm around my waist and held me back. "You don't attack a witch!" he scolded me.

"Especially when you need something," Celeste added.

I held my breath, forcing my boiling rage to taper down to a simmer, forcing myself to stop fantasizing about battering her to the floor. The tension slowly left my body. Kit must have felt me relax, because he slowly removed his arm. I glared at her and stalked into the house.

The interior walls were dark. If there were other doors, I couldn't see them. Candles strewn around the room barely illuminated a dark flagstone floor.

All I *could* see was one large room lined with shelves holding jars of dried herbs, small crystals, and metal shavings. More shelves held things that I looked away from the second I glimpsed them: eyeballs, hearts, teeth, tongues, other organs. Only two windows pierced the room, and they were covered by heavy red curtains with gold lace sewn along the edges. A rug under the round stone table in the center of the room displayed the same pattern.

"You have poor taste no matter where you are," I snapped, turning to face Celeste as she let Kit and Axel into the house.

When she shut the door, Axel laid down next to it, unusually calm. Kit walked around the room like he was looking for possible traps. I knew that just *standing* in the room was a trap.

"Send me back!" I demanded.

"You don't like it here?" Celeste smirked and looked at Kit, her gaze caressing him from his head to his feet. "I would if I were you."

"Send me back right now!" I shouted.

She just chuckled.

"It's. Not. Funny," I ground out.

She sighed. "I'm not sending you back. If it's any consolation, I don't see what's so great about you, but then again, I haven't been spending very much time with you." Her gaze slanted to Kit. "But you must know—you wouldn't have brought her here if you didn't have an idea of what you're dealing with."

I stared at Kit, waiting for him to say something, anything that would hint at what she was talking about, but he only glanced at me before glaring at Celeste. That glare was clearly telling her to shut up.

"Someone tell me *what is going on!*" I shouted.

They both looked at me.

"You're worth more money than any beast out there, and

I plan on collecting," Celeste said. I could only stare, horrified, as Kit opened his mouth to speak but then froze. Celeste quickly held up a hand, turning it slightly. The next thing I knew, Kit was falling to the ground. Axel toppled over a second later.

"What did you do?!" I shouted. I rushed over to Kit and rolled him onto his back. For the first time since I'd met him, he looked peaceful.

"He's no longer needed." Celeste stated. She stepped close to me. I felt my body tense. She put her hands up in surrender. "Relax! They're just sleeping. And I'm not going to hurt you."

"What do you mean about me being worth more than any beast?" I asked as I slowly stood up.

Celeste chuckled. She walked over to the table and pulled back a wooden chair, plopping herself down and throwing her feet up. Her crystal-studded black boots went all the way up to her knees.

She looked at me and sent chills down my spine with her smile. "People have been looking for you for years. Every year, the price of finding you gets higher and higher. You wouldn't believe how many realms I visited looking for you!"

I felt my jaw clenching. "You did all of that to send me *where* exactly?"

Celeste smirked. "Back to your parents."

The blood drained from my face. This couldn't be happening! I didn't want this, not anymore. Sure, I used to always think about what I would say when I found them. *If* I found them. Would I be happy or angry or sad? Or would I feel nothing? Finally, I'd reached a point that I'd stopped thinking about them at all. I couldn't. It was the only way I could keep going. *And she says she's going to* force *me into seeing them? I won't do it. I can't!*

"No!" Celeste's voice broke me out of my trance. My eyes

refocused on her, watching her bolt up out of her chair. "No, no, no, no, no!" She looked around the room like she was frantically searching for something. Something that was circling her. Something that I couldn't see.

"What?" I asked. She looked at me fearfully. I was sure she hadn't felt fear in a very long time. The ground under us started to shake as the candles' flames rose higher. "What is that?"

"This can't be happening! You can't be here!" Celeste half-shouted, half-sobbed. Blood starting to drip from her eyes like tears. "All my hard work for *nothing!*" When she looked at me again, her white eyes were slowly turning a deep red, like they were filling with blood. "He's coming for you."

"Who?"

Celeste started to laugh manically. "You'll know when he comes." Her laugh got harder and louder. The candle flames grew, blazing. Blood streamed down her face. She looked up, letting it streak down her cheeks and her neck. Blood slid down under her dress.

She fell to the ground with a loud thud. My breath froze as silence filled the room. It was a deathly silence, one that sent pain up shooting from my feet up through my body. I felt like I was standing over a roaring fire. I wanted to scream, but nothing came out.

Maisey... Maisey... Maisey...

I clapped my hands over my ears. The candles blew out and darkness overtook the room. "Stop it, stop it, stop it!" I begged the nonexistent voice. I fell to my knees.

The voice got stronger and louder. *Maisey... Maisey... Maisey...*

* * *

My body chilled. I didn't realize my eyes were closed until I opened them. But that didn't make a difference—it was just as dark with my eyes open as it had been when they were closed. "Hello?" I called out desperately. "What's happening to me?"

Red light surrounded me. My body tingled. A voice spoke. "You've felt that before—the power." Chills ran up my spine as the words punched through me.

"I don't know what you're talking about..."

Suddenly, the scene changed. I was standing by the bar in the inn. The man stood in front of me again. My hand swung up in a way I had no control over, smacking the bottle against his head and shattering it into pieces.

"The fight at the inn," the voice went on inexorably. "You hit that man with a bottle."

"I had to!"

The scene shifted, and I was standing over the man in Beatrice's home. I was plunging the dagger into the man. No matter how hard I tried to stop myself, my hand kept pushing. I could hear his skin parting and giving way for the dagger to go deeper into his body.

"You killed those men," the voice told me.

Everything vanished. A sob tore out of me. "I don't know what happened! I wasn't trying to kill them!" Tears streamed down my cheeks.

"You can't control it. I can help you."

I shook my head, my heart pounding. "No! I want out!" My voice strengthened, becoming demanding. "GET OUT OF MY HEAD!!" I roared in a way I hadn't known was possible.

I WAS BACK in Celeste's house. I stumbled to my feet, seeing that Kit and Axel were both still asleep, sprawled across the floor. I walked over to one of the narrow windows and pulled back the curtain. The edge of the moon barely peeked out from behind the clouds. Hours seemed to have passed since we'd stepped foot into this hell house.

I saw something else in the window, something that made my heart stop: two red eyes staring back at me. They radiated a kind of power I didn't want to feel or even think about.

I wanted those terrifying eyes to go away, but I quickly realized that they wouldn't...

...because they were mine.

CHAPTER 8

I found myself sitting by the wall, away from the sleeping forms of Kit and Axel and the dead body of Celeste. I held my knees close to my chest and let my forehead rest on them. My body ached. I just sat there, listening to the hard rainfall and the distant sound of thunder. I couldn't move; I couldn't risk getting a look at myself. I didn't even move when I heard a whine from Axel and a groan from Kit.

Kit cursed. I heard him stand up. "We need to go." I knew he was talking to me, but I didn't say a word. "Maisey! Will you get up?" He formed it as a question, but there was no asking in his tone—it held only annoyance.

"I can't get it to stop," I finally mumbled.

Kit sighed. "Can't get what to stop?"

I looked up at him, letting him see the red glow in my eyes. "I can't get it to stop."

Kit tried not to look worried, but his eyes gave him away. "What the hell happened?" Kit got down on one knee, lightly grabbed my chin, and peered into my eyes.

"It doesn't matter." I shook my head, dislodging his hand.

Kit stood again, "We need to go."

"So that you can lie to me again?"

"I have not lied to you."

My tone started to take on an edge. "But you haven't told me the whole truth! Which, you know, is the same as lying. That's why you don't like me asking questions. She said you knew there was something wrong with me!"

"And you're going to believe *her*?" He managed to indicate Celeste without looking at her.

I scoffed. *He* was the one looking insulted? As if *I* were the one keeping secrets? "I believed the look in your eyes when she brought it up." I pushed myself up, using the wall as a lever. I could feel the ground shifting under me. "You didn't want her to talk about it because you weren't sure if you were going to tell me. You *knew* there was something wrong and you didn't say a word! And you expect me to trust you?"

Kit let out a deep, frustrated breath. I was prepared for him to start yelling at me, to put up a fight. To make my anger worth it. Instead, he just let his head fall forward and sighed. Not a sigh of defeat, but one of regret. "Jasper and I went to go see a woman named Mangda. She's blind in this world, but when she looks through the veil between worlds, she can see everything. I went to her because—well, because I thought there was more to you. I wasn't sure what, I swear. But she got too close..." He trailed off.

"What happened?"

Kit finally looked over at Celeste's body. "That. Whatever it was, that same thing melted Mangda from the inside out."

"Did she say anything important?" I asked, not wanting to think about the poor woman's demise.

Kit shook his head. "Only that the disturbance in the dark forest was the start of the prophecy."

That just made things more confusing. "What prophecy?"

"I don't know." He looked back at me. "That's everything I know. I promise."

All I could think about was Cece and all that crap she'd been trying to tell me. Her words played through my mind like a movie that I couldn't pause even though I desperately wanted to. "She said she wanted to send me back to my parents. That the price for getting me back to them was always rising."

Kit tensed up. "Damn it!"

"This is the part where you share." My tone was stern and demanding. I hoped it would be hard for him to argue with me.

He just looked at me steadily. "I think I know who your parents are."

Panic rose through me like a tidal wave. "No."

"Maisey—"

"No!" I shook my head, stopping him from saying anything else. "I spent my whole life trying to be able to accept that my parents didn't want me! And now you want me to just go knock on their door and act like I haven't spent my entire life alone?" I slumped against the wall and slid back down to the floor.

Kit sat down next to me, sprawling his legs out in front of him. "You don't have to go to them. I'm not going to make you do something you don't want to do."

I just nodded, letting silence fall between us. Silence filled with anger and panic. Those were mainly coming from me, of course.

"What's it like?" Kit finally asked. "Maine, I mean?"

That surprised me. "Why do you ask?"

Kit lifted a shoulder. "I've never been anywhere else."

That was a good question for somebody like me who'd bounced everywhere. I can't even remember how I got to

Maine. I do remember that living in multiple states in my car wasn't the highlight of my life, though.

I shrugged. "Maine is the only place where I've felt safe. My last foster family—the people that took care of me for three years before I aged out of the system—live in Maine and staying there meant I didn't have to worry about being a scared eighteen-year-old without a family."

"What happened to them?"

I felt my heart crack in my chest. "They died. There was an accident—a fire. No one made it out." I rested my head back the wall, letting my eyelids get heavy and my emotions fall into the background of my mind.

* * *

A LIGHT BREEZE HIT ME, prompting me to open my eyes. I was sitting on a stone bench near a crystal-blue pond. I didn't recognize my surroundings, but I didn't care. A sense of peacefulness filled the air. Swans and ducks floated on the pond; bright, vibrant flowers grew at the pond's edges. Something was shining from the bottom of the pond. Crystals, maybe?

A presence was standing behind me. "Where am I?" I asked.

"After what happened, I thought you would want to be somewhere peaceful."

My heart stalled out in my chest as the hairs on my body stood up. I knew that voice. I felt the presence sit down on the other end of the bench and forced myself to look at him.

His appearance stunned me. He had almond skin and a sculpted face, light brown eyes with gold flecks in them, and short but thick hair that was just long enough for a few strands to fall over his forehead. He was dressed in a black shirt and pants and wore a gold cloak. The cloak had a snake embroidered along its edges; it looked like it was slithering up the fabric.

He wasn't what I'd expected, which was even more terrifying. "You're the voice." I spoke.

He just stared at the pond, apparently in some sort of trance.

I opened my mouth to speak, but he spoke instead. "This is just the form I'm taking so as not to cause you fear."

"Fear? You didn't care before. Why care now?"

He looked over at me with incredibly intense eyes. His gaze made me feel shaken to the core. "You're a special girl, Maisey. Very few have ever been able to reject my power."

"Who are you?"

He chuckled, looking away from me. "I have a lot of names."

"That still doesn't answer my question."

"You're not ready yet, but you're going to need me."

I stood up from the bench, shaking my head. "I'm not here to dance around whatever you have planned. I don't need you! I already have one infuriating man to deal with. I don't need another one!"

"Until you do. You will know where to find me." His smirk sent chills down my spine. I didn't want him to know how afraid I was, but I felt like he could sense it.

* * *

MY EYES SHOT OPEN. I was back in Celeste's house. A rage filled me, and this time, I couldn't stop myself from being overwhelmed by it. Nor did I want to. *This is all her fault! All this magic and these objects... They ruined my life!* I wanted it all to break. I wanted all of it to shatter under my rage. And that's what happened.

Every jar. Every crystal. Every skull. All of it shattered against the stone floor. The war raging inside of me matched the storm outside. Screams of anguish tore through the air: from all corners of the kingdom came screams from those who were unheard, those who were dying, those who were gone.

Gradually, I felt my hands gripping the stone table in the center of the room. My vision cleared as the rage left my body. The pounding in my ears subsided; I could finally hear Kit talking to me.

"Feel better?" he asked. I just shook my head. "I know where we can go to figure this out—my brother. He's been studying you for a long time and he'll know how to help us." Despite his hopeful statement, his voice was laced with dread.

I finally looked at Kit and saw him staring at the ground. "You don't sound excited."

"My brother isn't...well, put together. Hasn't been for a long time..."

CHAPTER 9

We set off for wherever we were going in silence. The silence stretched on—every time I tried to talk to Kit about his brother, I was met with silence. Every time I tried to talk about myself, I was met with silence. Every time I talked about the weather, I was met with silence.

But he wasn't actively ignoring me—when I sank into the silence and listened closely, I could hear him mumbling under his breath. I just couldn't make out the words.

Finally, we reached a house hidden deep within the trees. A slight clearing circled it. Axel stayed underneath the tree farthest away from the house, hidden from anyone but us.

Grass had started growing up the side of the house, and nothing in its vicinity looked purposely cultivated. If Kit hadn't so clearly known where he was going, I would have thought the place was abandoned.

"Watch your step," Kit warned me. "Stay exactly behind me." He led me through the tall grass, following an unseen and jagged path.

"What do you mean?" I asked, trying to see what he was looking for.

"He doesn't like visitors, so he sets traps."

"Oh, good! And here I was afraid my experience with the Hell Beast trap was going to be the only one!"

Kit ignored me and kept going. He made sure I was standing behind him when he opened the door.

"You're not going to knock?" I blurted out. "But you said he doesn't like visitors, right?" I did my best to keep my voice down.

Kit scoffed. "He's not awake."

I could only follow him as he used his weight to push open the door, shoving aside whatever was placed behind it. A strong, musty smell barreled out of the house. I quickly covered my nose and tried not to gag.

Under the mess of papers, clothes, bottles, bottles, and even more bottles was a very unconscious body lying on the floor on top of even more clothes. I wasn't completely convinced he was even alive as Kit gave the body a swift kick. "Get up!"

The body groaned, struggling to push itself up. The man was lean and shorter than Kit, without any obvious tattoos and with very bare legs.

I quickly turned, hearing a curse from Kit. "Put this on!" Kit told him.

Another string of curses ensued; this time uttered by a new voice. "Who the hell is that?!" I still wasn't looking at him, but I knew Kit's brother was staring at me.

When I turned back around, I saw that he had thankfully put on some pants. That didn't make him look any better, though—his long brown hair was wild and knotted, matching the long beard he probably hadn't trimmed in weeks.

"Tobyn, meet Maisey," was Kit's only introduction. His next words were directed at me. "Watch yourself!"

Kit walked past his brother to get a better look at the chaos. I craned my neck, scanning the room, but I didn't move. It wasn't hard to see that while Kit's house was cluttered, Tobyn's was downright dirty.

Tobyn stared at me with a strange look on his face, like I was a painting with a hidden message he would see if he stared long enough. He stepped closer to me, narrowing his eyes. "You don't look like a whore."

"Thanks," I said dryly.

He walked away from me without a second look, rummaging through the bottles that were sitting on a table until he found one that was half full. He downed it like it was water. "I told you not to come back here!" he told Kit a second before he threw the bottle onto the floor. The mess covering the floor kept the bottle from breaking.

Kit looked at him with a hard, unreadable expression, one I hadn't seen even amidst the dangers of the dark forest. "Trust me, if I'd had any other option, I wouldn't be here. I enjoy your company as much as you enjoy mine."

"Then what do you want?"

"I want to know about the day the princess went missing."

Tobyn cursed, shaking his head. He stumbled to the couch. "Why would I want to talk about *that*?" He rested his arms on his legs, staring down at his hands. "That little shit ruined my life."

"She was an infant." Kit rolled his eyes as he walked to the couch to stand over his brother. He crossed his arms over his chest. "Now explain."

"Piss off." Tobyn tried to brush him off, but Kit just continued to stare at him. "Why do you want to know?"

"That's not your concern."

"If you want me to relive the worst day of my life, then it is."

Kit didn't waver. "Talk."

Tobyn shot to his feet. "Not until you tell me why!" He glared at his brother. From his assertive stance, I realized that Tobyn was the older one. Tobyn's gaze fell over Kit's shoulder, stopping on me. "No. No, no, no, *no!*"

Tobyn lunged towards me, but Kit quickly braced his hands on his brother's chest, pushing him back down onto the couch and holding him there. "Don't—"

"You did this! You and your parents ruined my life!" Tobyn screamed, still struggling against Kit's grip.

"Calm down!" Kit shouted. He finally got Tobyn to pry his eyes away from me.

"Why the hell would you bring *her* here?" Tobyn spat at him. "Why would you bring her into my home just so she can look down on me *again?*"

"Maybe I should wait outside," I quickly interjected.

Kit shot me an inscrutable look. "No." His gaze went back to Tobyn. "It's not her fault that you failed. You were always trying to please the man who hated you more than he hated me, and he cast *me* out along with the animals." Kit snorted and loosened his grip on his brother. "Now, for the first time in years, make yourself useful."

Both men stared at each other and apparently came to a silent agreement. Kit finally let his brother go.

"I'm going to need a drink," Tobyn finally muttered.

"Me, too," I mumbled under my breath.

Kit picked a bottle up from the floor and handed it to his brother, then sat down on the cluttered coffee table. He seemed unfazed by the surrounding junk.

I cleared off a rocking chair as best I could, moving the papers and clothing stacked on it to the floor. The chair was a good distance from Tobyn. I think he preferred that, too, because he seemed to calm down.

Tobyn took a swallow from the bottle. "I joined the war as soon as I got the chance—thought it was better than being in that house. I was going to fight next to the King! His lead knight took me under his wing! I didn't think anything could be better."

A small smile spread across his face. "And then we won! Do you know what it's like to beat the odds? To think you were going to die far across the sea but then you win instead?" A proud chuckle punctuated his words. "After the war, I was invited to join the Castle Knights. My tasks were minor until I was done with the formal training, of course. But all of it was a dream come true! The castle, the people, the women. One had the best p—"

"Focus." Kit quickly cut him off, leaving my imagination to fill in the blank.

Tobyn scoffed, taking another drink. "I'd forgotten how enjoyable you are."

"What changed?" I asked.

He finally looked at me again. Hate lingered in his eyes. "You. I was on your guard that night. The nanny left the nursery, saying you were asleep. Nothing seemed to be wrong, but when the nanny came back in the middle of the night, you were gone."

His voice got even colder. "And it was *my* fault. *I* was thrown into a cell because they swore, I had to know something. Babies don't just blow away with the wind, they said."

This wave of guilt ran through me. "So, they kicked you out of the Castle Knights."

He finished off the bottle. "Yeah. I guess after weeks of me being in that horrible cell, they realized that if I'd had something to say, I would have told them."

Another silence filled the room. Kit was the one to break it. "You're lying."

Tobyn glared at him. "How would you know? You weren't there!"

"I didn't need to be there—I know there's no way they let you go out of the kindness of their hearts. Why did they *really* let you go? If you don't tell us the truth, I'll slam your head into the table."

I winced, thinking that was a bit harsh, but Tobyn's expression softened. He sighed and tossed the bottle onto the ground. "I used to hear the guards talking about a prophecy."

Kit was relentless. "What prophecy?"

"You think they told me all the details?" Tobyn laughed as if the question was some kind of lighthearted joke. "All I heard was rumors. The guards said the simple existence of the prophecy kept the King's throne from being challenged."

I'd opened my mouth to speak when a howl filled the air. Kit instantly headed to the door. The sound of thudding hoofbeats came next, prompting Tobyn to follow him. He only slightly stumbled.

Kit stepped out of the cabin, followed by Tobyn and then me. We immediately found ourselves encircled by men on horseback. Most were dressed in silver armor that was tinted red along the edges of their breastplates. Long red fabric flowed from their shoulders and down their backs. The centers of their chestplates were emblazoned with a...fire-bird? I wasn't entirely sure.

But five men weren't wearing that armor. One of them rode his horse closer to us. He and the four others were dressed in black armor trimmed with gold. A gold snake adorned their chests.

This particular man had short brown hair and wrinkles lining his clean-shaved face. His light blue eyes contrasted sharply with his dark armor. A scar traveled from the side of his mouth all the way up to his ear. "Their Royal Majesties demand that everyone return to the castle," he called out. "The girl rides with me."

Before I could protest, another man came forward. "You forget yourself," he said sharply. He was around the other man's age, but this one was bald, with blonde stubble. "You came as a courtesy for Lady Anna, but you aren't a royal guard. The girl rides with me." He looked at the three of us. "Tobyn."

Tobyn slightly nodded at him. "Jedediah."

Jedediah's green eyes moved towards me. "Come with me, miss." His voice was kind, but I'd been fooled by supposedly nice men before. Noticing my hesitation, he looked back at his men. "Give me two of your horses," he commanded. Two were immediately brought forward.

Tobyn tried to argue, saying something about there being little point in him going along. "I take no accountability for the girl or my brother," he said defiantly.

That got an eyeroll from Kit and zero response from the armored men—Tobyn was urged onto one horse while I rode behind Kit on the other. The soldiers bunched themselves around us as we rode, blocking us from galloping away. I wrapped my arms around Kit's waist and pressed my ear up against his back, listening to the sound of his steady, calm heartbeat while I watched the trees move past us.

Birds flew over towards us, winging their way furiously along as though they were doing their best to fly away from something. The sky was bright despite the sun being hidden behind the clouds.

Abruptly, the dirt road we were on deposited us onto a stone road. "Where are we going?" I asked Kit in a hushed tone. I wanted him to say something even if it was just to tell me he didn't know.

But before he could answer, I caught a glimpse of something that made my stomach drop: an imposing stone castle stood in the distance, rising so tall that it looked as though it was touching the sky. It took everything I had not to jump off the horse and start running away, but there were soldiers all around us. Besides, even if I got past them, where would I go? There was only one place I *could* go.

No matter how much I didn't want to.

CHAPTER 10

We rode the horses down a path to the side of the castle, where an awning stretched over a corridor with multiple arches and a door at each end. The second the horses stopped, and we dismounted, the mood shifted.

A large hand forcefully grabbed one of mine. Kit yelled, but guards aggressively grabbed him and Tobyn as well. "It'll be fine!" I yelled back at Kit. I didn't like the way the guards were eyeing him. "You've done enough for me. Just do what they say!"

The armored man, dressed in black, who'd been the first to talk to me pulled me through one of the doors. "Some power there, if I do say so myself," he cooed into my ear. "Too bad you won't see him again."

My heart pounded as we walked through an empty hall. Just like the exterior, the interior of the castle was made of a light-colored stone. The hall was lit by an occasional window and candles burning in sconces along the walls. Paintings and sculptures were scattered along the corridor. Most of the paintings depicted landscapes, but many of the wooden doors we passed had firebirds painted on them.

Two guards stood outside the biggest door I'd seen so far. They opened it and I was pushed inside. This floor was different—it wasn't just flagstones. Instead, a mosaic of a battle scene sprawled out under our feet, illuminated by multiple chandeliers blazing with candles. Two oversized thrones stood at the far end of the chamber, both hewn of a dark-colored wood and lined with red cushions.

Only one other person was in the room, and she was sitting on one of the thrones. Her skin was as pale as mine. Long, curly black hair hung over her shoulders. Her eyes were so dark that I was sure they were black, and her black dress exactly followed the curves of her body—its long sleeves clung to her arms and a deep V neckline traveled nearly down to her navel. Diamonds hung within the V, sparkling brightly. Even though she was physically small, she carried herself with a great deal of power.

"You know I have seen many traitors in this room," she said to me. "But you have put in the most effort." She smirked. "I appreciate that."

"I'm not a traitor!" I protested. "I don't even belong here!"

"I agree with you." She looked at the soldier next to me and nodded. He finally let go of me and left the room.

The woman turned back to me. "My sister is…a fragile woman. Always has been. Mother used to say, 'Grace is simple at heart. Worry plagues her; love will be her downfall.' Crazy woman, but she knew what she was babbling about."

She put her hands on the arms of the throne, then pushed herself up and walked towards me. "In the end, her love for my father is what killed her. Funny, isn't it? To be so worried that your child will love too much and then your own heart being the one who betrays you." Her chuckle made me want to disappear into the mosaic under my feet. My discomfort was clear to her, I could tell. She enjoyed it. I was only supposed to listen, not speak.

Her smirk finally disappeared once she stood in front of me. Fear flooded through me in a way I'd never felt before. "But her heart is my responsibility! And people like you… Well, you'll be of little concern even before the sun goes down."

"But I didn't do anything!" I said weakly.

"Well, what is it they say? Rumors kill; facts disappear." Her eyes shifted from black to a glowing deep purple.

My heart raced faster, every beat feeling like it was hitting my breastbone. My hand instinctively covered my chest like I could keep my heart from shooting out of my body. Her eyes peered deeper into me, and I started to feel an overwhelming weight crushing me and bringing me to my knees.

Suddenly, the door opened. The weight vanished, leaving me gasping for air. "What are you doing?" a voice asked. It was laced with panic.

"I'm simply handling a problem," she answered crisply. "Maybe I should remind you that this is what I do."

"You question them, yes, but you have no right to kill them!" the voice snapped. "I'll bring her to the testing room."

I felt hands grab my arms and help me up. "Come, child." The female voice was calm and light. It drifted across my ears like a fresh breeze.

I looked at the woman next to me and instantly felt at ease. She had long blue hair that matched her sparkling eyes. The same color was echoed by her loose dress that hung softly against her skin. Every part of her looked purposeful, even the torn hem of her dress. Her bare feet were covered with dirt. Although she looked younger than me, I felt so small in front of her. Still, her aura was one I admired rather than feared.

I ignored the imposing woman and let the kind one take

my hand and guide me out of the room. "Who are you?" I asked as we walked together down the hall.

She let go of my hand. "Cordelia," she told me with a smile. "The lead fairy in charge here at the castle."

Somehow that didn't shock me. "What do you do?"

"Keep the peace, regulate magic inside of the castle, and keep the balance outside of it." She led me through two doors that opened with just a slight movement of her hands.

This room was smaller than the last. Its walls were covered with wallpaper that looked like red marble. A large rectangular table stood in the center of the room and arched windows rose on either side of the arched glass door. At the end of the table a tray held an array of glasses and bottles.

"What is this place?" I asked as I walked around the table.

"It's one of the minor meeting rooms, not one used by the King or Queen." She walked to the tray. "Would you like a drink?" With a quick motion of her hand, she set both glasses on the table in front of me.

I quickly shook my head. The calm I had felt was suddenly replaced by troubling thoughts. *What happened to Kit?* Panic wormed its way into my veins. If they thought *I* was a traitor, what did they think of him? And where was he being kept?

"Interesting." Cordelia's gentle voice broke me out of my worsening thoughts.

"What?"

"Normally my effects last longer—even after I'm gone sometimes. But you..." She cocked her head, staring at me. "What took you out of it?"

I hesitated to tell her. If she liked me, she could help me, but if she didn't, she could make everything worse. Still, what other choice did I have? I decided to ask a question of my own. "Where are the men I came here with?"

"They're being held until we decide what to do with you."

Cordelia waved at a chair, and it obediently scooted out for her. She sat. "What do they mean to you?"

"One is…somewhat a friend. The other is my friend's brother."

In response, she motioned a chair to slide out for me. "I got a message about you from Cecelia—that's how I was able to find you. What happened to her? She's not the type of person to just vanish without collecting, and she expected a large payment."

I looked down at my hands. "She's dead." Images of blood spilling down her face filled my mind. I could still hear her chilling laughter as she died, intertwined with an edge of pain. "I couldn't see what was attacking her, but I think she could. She…she was bleeding *everywhere*." I forced myself to look up at Cordelia.

She didn't look fazed one bit. "Well, there's a test to see if she's right." Rather surprisingly, she reached out and used her hands to fill one of the glasses.

"What happens if I don't take the test?"

She chuckled and sipped, then paused as I stared flatly at her. "You're serious?" she finally asked. I just nodded. She set the glass down with a sigh. "Then Lady Anna will have you labeled a traitor and an impostor, and you will be executed before the sun sets. You've already seen what she can do. What she *will* do."

A sudden, horrible pressure fell onto my shoulders. "I don't want to die! But I'm *not* their daughter," I managed to say.

Cordelia pursed her lips and circled her fingertips over her glass, idly moving the water. "I'm going to offer you a choice. I will test you, and if you fail, I'll send you home before Lady Anna even finds out the results."

My eyebrows pinched together in confusion. "Why would you do that?"

"I hate witches. If you're here by the request of—of one of them, then it wasn't your choice." I could tell she was censoring herself.

I tilted my head, considering. If this Lady Anna had truly wanted to test me, she would have. Unless she needed me to agree to be tested. But why would anyone *ask* me to take the test? Presumably the King and Queen needed to know whether or not I was their daughter. Why negotiate?

The pressure started to fade as I realized the power I held. *There's no way out of this test, but I'm not the one who needs help,* I thought. *Then again, if Cordelia sends me back, what will happen to Kit?* Aloud, I said, "I'll do it, but I want you to let my friends go first."

Cordelia shook her head. "That's not my choice."

"Then I want to see the King and Queen."

"That's not part of the deal."

"If I don't take the test, they run the risk that someone might decide to kill me before they can figure out if I'm their daughter or not. Is that a choice you want to make for them?"

Cordelia chuckled again and stood. "You're smart. It's never fun making a deal when someone doesn't know the cards they hold. Wait here." She waved the door open, then walked out. The door shut behind her.

I let out a big breath of relief. Nausea flooded through me and made me feel slightly dizzy. To try to clear my head, I got up and walked over to the glass door that led out to the balcony. I slipped through the door and went to stand at the balcony's edge, lightly gripping the white stone railing. Purple flowers twined through the rails and brushed against my fingers. The sky was a beautiful light blue, the sun was bright, and there wasn't a single cloud in the sky.

Despite the beauty surrounding me—or because of it— goosebumps ran down my arms. I thought about the people dying in the sick tents outside of the dark forest, cowering underneath gray clouds. The rulers here were so worried about me, yet they didn't seem to be worried about the people they were supposed to be looking after. What did that say about them?

* * *

CORDELIA RETRACED our route through the halls, back to the stone archways. "Wait here," Cordelia told me before reentering the chamber.

It wasn't long before another door opened and a guard led Kit and Tobyn towards me. Kit looked relieved, but Tobyn was sweating and shaking. "How did you get us out?" Kit asked.

Tobyn cut me off before I could speak. "Who cares?" He nervously rubbed his hands together. "I'm leaving!"

Tobyn tried to walk away, but Kit grabbed the back of his shirt, stopping him. "What did it cost you?" Kit asked me.

"They're going to test me to see if I'm the princess. If I fail, they'll send me back to Maine."

Kit kept his eyes on me. "I'll stay with you."

I quickly shook my head. "No, I can't ask you to do that."

"You didn't ask."

"You've already risked so much for me. You don't need to do it anymore."

"I gave you my word that I would get you home. I'm staying." His tone was final.

"Well, I'm not," Tobyn said just as firmly. "Not that either of you asked."

Kit rolled his eyes at his brother. "Yet you're still here."

"Consider me gone." Tobyn gave us a small smirk before walking away.

I clasped my hands together tightly, trying to calm myself. A part of me wanted to admit how scared I was. How I couldn't decide if knowing was better than *not* knowing. But before I could get out another word, the doors opened again, and Cordelia was standing there smiling at me. "We're ready."

No turning back now. No running and praying I could stay hidden long enough to make it back home. I'd made my choice.

CHAPTER 11

Cordelia walked me deep into the castle, leading me up a flight of stairs to an arched, solid wooden door. It swung open before she could even knock.

Cordelia was still smiling, but now her smile looked forced. "Tasar, are you here?" she called out softly.

A man—Tasar, presumably—appeared in the doorway, his hands braced against the sides of it. His brown eyes bored into me. He was thin and tall, with white hair and a tattoo of a band around his neck.

"Is that her?" Tasar whispered.

"Tasar!" Cordelia's voice was jarringly stern. "Is *she* here? Did you tell her?"

Tasar nodded, pulling his eyes away from me. "I—I told her. I told her just as soon as I got word that you wanted to do the test. She didn't answer my first message, so I kept sending them. She finally replied a minute ago—she told me she'd end her vacation when the gods came down and dragged her away."

Cordelia let out a deep breath.

"I know what to do," Tasar assured her.

Cordelia ever so slightly nodded before looking back at me. "I will leave you alone in the very...capable hands of Tasar."

"I'd feel better if you sounded more believable," I couldn't help saying.

She just nodded again and retreated down the steps.

Panic rippled through me as Tasar motioned me into the room. Even though I was pretty sure I could bolt down the stairs and outrun him, I didn't want to spend my entire life running away. I'd done enough of that already.

I took a deep breath and walked past Tasar. Unlike the other rooms I'd seen, this one was small and cluttered. Tables were stacked with books, various liquids, and glass cylinders, and one wall was completely covered with bookshelves that were halfway filled. Plants stood before two large windows that had three metal bars running horizontally across them. I didn't find those bars comforting.

"Eventually, I'll possess every healing book in the world." I jumped at the sound of Tasar's voice and quickly turned around. "Sorry—I didn't mean to scare you," he apologized.

I sighed. "It's fine. I just... I just want to get this over with."

He pointed to a chair by the table. "Have a seat. I'll prepare what we need." He proceeded to scrounge around the room, holding a piece of paper in his hand and mumbling under his breath. Eventually, he walked back to me with a vial of a red liquid, a rolled-up piece of paper, and a small knife. He set everything on the table and looked up at me. "I know this looks worrying, but it's not too bad, I promise."

"Then why do you have a weapon?" I looked at the knife.

Tasar chuckled. "It's barely going to hurt. We took samples of the King's and Queen's blood and spellbound them together. I'm going to dip one end of the enchanted parchment in their combined blood and dab a few drops of your blood on the other end. If you are in fact their daughter, the blood will merge. If you're not, the paper will explode. Nothing serious, but there could be a bit of fire."

I bit my lip, then finally asked what was bothering me. "Why did Cordelia spend so much time persuading me to agree to the test?"

He gave me a half-smile. "It only works if the person agrees. There are other tests that are... Well, let's just say they're troublesome." He rolled the parchment out on the table, placing a small stone on each corner to hold it down. "Those tests don't require consent, but then again, fewer people have claimed to be the princess lately. Last I heard, it's been four months' time since anyone claimed to be her."

"Well, *I'm* not claiming that."

He gave me a strange look. "Then why come to the castle?"

"Knights showed up and didn't give me a choice." I remembered what I'd seen depicted throughout the castle. "Why are there firebirds everywhere?"

Tasar laughed. "It's a phoenix, but I prefer the idea of a firebird." He picked up the vial and poured half of its contents on one end of the parchment, then held out his hand to me. "Remember, I can't make you do this," he reminded me.

My mind took me back to the night of the soul sucker and how much pain I'd felt when Kit had had to cut into my thigh. "Can I do it?" I asked.

Tasar nodded, turning the knife in his hand to offer me the hilt. "Just cut your palm and squeeze some blood onto the parchment."

I took the silver knife from him and held up my palm. Before I could think about it any longer, I held my breath and quickly slid the knife across my palm, making a shallow cut. I ignored the burning pain and squeezed my fist over the parchment. After several drops of my blood had stained it, Tasar turned my palm up and wrapped it in a black cloth.

"Now we watch," he said. Neither of our eyes left the parchment.

I didn't know what I wanted to happen. Was there any way out of this situation that *wasn't* going to crush every part of me?

One thing was certain: I wasn't ready to see the blood-stains begin to move from the ends of the parchment to pool together in the center. Then, suddenly, flames engulfed the entire paper and turned it to ash in an eyeblink.

Tasar and I sat in silence as flames ate up the entire sheet of parchment. Then they died out as quickly as they had started.

"What was *that*?" I shouted, breaking the unbearable silence. "You said it would set itself on fire if I failed or that the blood would merge if I passed. It just did *both*!"

Tasar sat blinking at the table, his lips forming mumbled sounds. "I don't know... I haven't seen a positive test before!" He rushed over to a heavy tome sitting on a corner table and started flipping through it, still mumbling.

"What are you doing?" I asked. He continued to flip. The more he didn't talk, the more my fear rose inside of me. *"What are you doing?"* I repeated more loudly.

"Trying to find more information about this test," he answered absentmindedly.

"How can you *not* know?" I used my shaking arms to push myself up from the chair.

"This test has been done before, of course, but never with results like that..." His mouth continued to move, but his voice died out.

I wanted to tell him that I couldn't hear him, but my voice was gone, too. I only heard silence—I couldn't even hear my own heart beating. Seconds later, the entire room tilted to its side. Then darkness replaced it.

* * *

THE FIRST THING I was able to hold onto was the pain radiating throughout my body. I tried to open my eyes, but I couldn't see anything. "You're okay," I heard. The voice was distant, but as my eyes started to focus, I was able to make out Tasar standing over me, waving his hand in my face. "Although you did hit your head pretty hard on the way down."

I sighed, flinching at a stinging in my head as I slowly pushed myself up.

"Is your magic unstable?" Tasar asked.

I frowned up at him. "What?"

Tasar shifted from kneeling to sitting down. "Since you've been here, have you had any sudden outbursts? Emotionally or maybe physically?"

I hesitated to answer him. "I guess..."

"Did you have magic in the world you were in before?"

My brows furrowed. "How did you know I was somewhere else?"

Tasar scoffed. "If you'd been here, they would have found you."

"No, they didn't have...magic...where I was."

Tasar's eyes widened. "So *that's* why there was fire!" he nearly shouted. He shot to his feet.

"Why are you yelling?" I asked.

"I'll show you!" he said excitedly as he started scrambling around the room.

"Okay, okay, okay..." I waited and watched him.

He didn't say another word until he had gotten a candle and a glass candle snuffer and set them down in front of me.

"When a person is born with magic, they have what we call a 'source' inside of them," he said. He picked up a match and lit the candle. "As the person grows up, the source becomes bigger. When that person lives in a world with magic, the source grows steadily and is able to be controlled, but if you throw that same person into a world without magic, the source starts to die even though that person's body will struggle to keep it going."

My eyebrows were creeping up as he covered the candle and watched the flame dwindle. "But if you throw that person into a world that has magic without taking *any* precautions first," He removed the snuffer and let the flame lick upwards again. "The source becomes unstable and can grow wildly. That person's body—in this case, *your* body— will struggle to keep the source contained."

I stared at the candle flame. "So, before I kept passing out because I was dying…and now I pass out because I can't control the raging…uh…" I trailed off.

"Magic, yes," he answered for me. "You have a hard time with that word, don't you?"

"I'm working on it." I briefly closed my eyes. "What do we do now?"

This time he was the one who paused. "I don't know," he finally said. "Which is rare, because I know a lot. I've read every book in this room"—he gestured at the bulging shelves —"and then some. No one knows how to handle this situation. No one else has survived for as long as you have."

I frowned at him. "So, you have ideas but no solutions."

He sighed. "The only thing we can do is wait and see what happens. We'll find someone who can teach you magic." He blew out the candle and got up to return it to its place on the shelf. "Hopefully we can retrain your powers before it comes."

"What's 'it'?"

He froze. "What?" he asked innocently.

"You said before 'it' comes. What's coming?"

He gave a slight shrug. "Why would you think something is coming?"

"My body might be struggling, but my hearing is fine," I said sharply. "What aren't you saying?"

He looked back at me, his hands moving up as if he were surrendering. "Why would I say anything?"

I suddenly remembered Tobyn saying that the guards had been talking about a prophecy. "Are you talking about the prophecy?"

Tasar's eyes narrowed. "How do you know about that? *I* certainly know nothing." He quickly turned away from me and seemed to be studying his shelves.

"You *do* know something!" I got up and stalked over to Tasar, following him as he hastily moved to the other side of his desk.

"Why would I say something if I have nothing more to say?"

I slammed my hands onto the desk, making him jump. "Stop answering my questions with more questions!"

Tasar pressed his lips together, struggling to maintain eye contact with me. "You're smart. I don't like that."

"Answer me."

Tasar sighed again; I could see his willpower draining away. "Workers found two objects when they were digging in the mines south of the castle's boundaries," he said grudgingly. "The pieces were carved out of a kind of diamond-like glass no one had seen before."

"Did they have writing on them?"

Tasar's silence spoke volumes.

"What did they say?" I pressed him.

Tasar looked down, shaking his head. "No one aside from Cordelia and your parents truly knows."

"But *you* know something."

"Just rumors." I stared at him; Tasar plopped himself down into a chair. "One was about the return of the princess. Supposedly."

"And the other?"

He shook his head again. "Has no merit."

"Tasar." My voice was as stern as Cordelia's had been.

He looked away from me. It looked like he wanted to say something, but his own body seemed to be stopping him. He fidgeted as I waited impatiently, then stood up again.

I quickly grabbed his arm and made him look at me. "I have to know!"

Tasar let out a breath. "'Hell walking on Neville.' That was what the other one had written on it."

My mind started racing in circles…until my tension all came vomiting out, covering the floor in front of me as well as poor Tasar's shoes. And mine.

I pulled my hair back and managed to catch my breath, panting and staring down at the vomit-stained ankle wrappings. "That's fine—I didn't like those anyway."

CHAPTER 12

Tasar cleaned me up before walking me back to the room I'd been in with Cordelia. This time, Kit was standing on the balcony. Tasar walked out and shut the door behind him.

Silence fell, but the moment I looked at Kit, I blurted out, "I passed." My voice cracked and my eyes started to burn with tears. The glass doors behind us blew open but somewhat surprisingly didn't shatter.

"Breathe!" Kit urged me. "Nothing good happens when you panic!"

I nodded and wiped my eyes.

"You just have to hang on," he said insistently. "And trust no one. I mean *no one*."

I took a deep breath. "I trust you. You're the only person I trust."

Kit put his hands on my arms, his brown eyes gazing into my own. "Well, then, believe me when I tell you this castle isn't safe. Not until we know who came after you."

"Just promise me that you won't leave me." A part of me

cursed myself for sounding so desperate, but I couldn't stop the words from coming out.

"I'm not going anywhere."

I nodded, then stepped closer to him, wrapping my arms around him and letting my head rest on his chest. His heartbeat was fast, but the warmth of his skin was calming. There was a sense of peace in it, a peace I wasn't used to. A peace I didn't know I had craved.

I pulled back, looking at him and about to speak. But before I could utter a word, a noise near the door stopped me. I quickly took a step away from Kit.

A man and a woman had walked into the room. Their glittering crowns quickly gave away their identities.

The King was older, with a full head of gray hair and a beard to match; he was tall and had pale skin and pale green eyes. *I looked more like him when I was sick,* I thought. A harsh scar ran down from his hairline to his right eye and stopped at the top of his cheek. His garments were shades of red, and he was wearing a gold necklace with a large cross dangling from it. Black gloves covered his hands.

The Queen was shorter than her husband—she was the same height as me, I noticed. Her intricately braided long blonde hair fell onto her shoulders and her skin was golden against the long-sleeved cream dress she wore. A square red crystal hung from her neck, resting over her heart. Her blue eyes scanned me intently. She looked like she was holding back what she wanted to say.

I understood and appreciated their hesitation.

The King cleared his throat, breaking the silence. "We know this must be a lot for you right now."

"But we also need to restore you to your birthright," the Queen quickly added with a small smile on her face.

"First things first! Rooms are being prepared for you and your friend," the King said somewhat stiffly.

"Unless you need one room," the Queen added.

"No, two is fine," Kit said from behind me.

I noticed the way her brow arched at his response, as if she were surprised he responded in the first place. It made me wonder when the last time she talked to one of her people. The Queen looked away from him and back at me. "I shall be arranging for you to learn about Nevillian history, your duties, and what will be expected of you in the future. And of course, you'll have to meet the lovely workers here in the castle and get to know the different regions in our control and the different houses of important—"

"Grace…" The King tried to stop her list of demands, but she seemed unfazed. My heart raced as I tried to keep up with my apparent new duties.

"You'll learn how to sit, dance, talk, eat, drink, even relax as a princess," she continued relentlessly. "You'll have daily tasks that I'll walk you through. And then of course you must learn how to control your magic. Tasar informed us of the effort you'll need to expend there—"

"Stop!" I shouted. My vision turned red. Everyone in the room went silent.

"How about some air?" I heard Kit ask over my shoulder. I quickly nodded and headed for the door.

"A knight will escort you," the Queen said hastily. That didn't slow me down—I didn't care how I got out of the castle, I just wanted out.

Kit and I hurried out of one of the many large doors and found ourselves in a grassy field. We kept going and soon neared a cliff. The scent of salt water filled my nose, calming my body and fully clearing my vision. I could hear the sound of waves crashing against the stone edge.

Kit didn't say a word—he just stood next to me and we watched the waves together. His warm hand brushed the top of mine.

Even though my heart was racing again, I didn't feel the chaos I had felt before. I turned my head to look at him. When he finally glanced away from the horizon and met my gaze, his dark brown eyes seemed softer than they ever had before.

"Kit…" My breath caught in my throat.

"There you are!" a cheerful voice sang out. We turned around and saw a short, round woman running towards us and waving her arms in the air. Her dark hair was pulled into a tight bun on the top of her head, and she wore a long black dress. An apron was tied over it.

"Aren't you beautiful?" she said as she neared us. She stepped closer to me and laid her cold hands on my cheeks, tears falling down her own. "I don't know why they wasted their time on those foolish tests! *I* could tell who you were from your eyes alone. I watched those eyes! I remember seeing those eyes every time I put you to bed."

"Who are you?" I quietly asked.

She quickly dropped her hands. "Oh, yes! I forgot that you wouldn't remember me." She chuckled and wiped away her tears. "I was your nanny. My name is Abbey. Come! I'll bring you to your rooms."

I just nodded and followed her back into the castle, Kit trailing behind us. The walls moved in a blur. Every hallway and turn started to make my brain hurt.

Abbey shooed Kit into his bedroom without a word and then ushered me down the hall. "I know it's a lot, but you'll get used to it."

"People keep saying that," I said doubtfully.

She smiled at me. "Normally you would be placed on a higher-level floor, but I figured you would want to be close to your friend." She opened the door at the end of the hallway and waited for me to step past her.

I held my breath as I stepped into the large room. And

when I say large, I mean *large*. As in, my apartment would have fit into it twice. A huge bed stood by one wall, its headboard adorned with beautiful carvings of flowers and trees. Shades of reds and whites danced across the walls, complementing the large round carpet in the center of the chamber. White blankets with phoenixes embroidered on them were draped over the bed.

"The white door to the left leads to the wardrobe, and on the right is the bath," Abbey told me.

I walked over to the white door and opened it, expecting a copious closet. I was shocked to instead see what I would call a lounge area, with three white couches set around a large coffee table. Racks upon racks of dresses and a full-length mirror were on one side of the room, and a vanity with far too many shelves of hair and face products stood on the other side.

But what shocked me most was looking at my reflection. I knew I was changing—I could feel it. For one thing, I wasn't fainting or feeling horrible chills or crushing exhaustion every hour. Still, standing there and looking in the mirror made me realize that not just the inside of me was changing.

My light green eyes no longer hid any pain. Loose waves of soft red hair had escaped from my ponytail, and even though it was messy and tangled, the rich color of it alone brought tears to my eyes.

"I'll have dinner brought up to you." Abbey's voice broke into my thoughts. I turned and nodded at her. She quickly curtsied and left.

Only silence accompanied me now. I was usually fine with silence; I usually never felt alone in it. Until now. This wasn't just being alone—this was a sort of cold silence.

But I was surrounded by beauty. It was overwhelming. Going from living in a shoebox to *this*?

Still, despite my luxurious chamber, I felt uneasy. All of

the expectations and questions the King and Queen had were unsettling, to say the least. Were they arguing about how to handle me? How to fix my temper? It's not like I'd treated them well during our brief first meeting.

I remembered what I'd always hoped for before. I used to pray that one day, my parents—no, my mom—would find me and tell me that she was sorry. Tell me that everything was going to be okay. That I would never be alone again.

And now I'm here. And all I can think about is how much I'll let them down. I can't do it. I can't handle all of that learning, all of those responsibilities, I thought desperately.

I'm just a waitress. I'm not a princess.

CHAPTER 13

I was sitting at the table on the balcony when my food arrived. I couldn't believe what was placed in front of me: a tower of strawberries, grapes, oranges, peaches, and kiwis; a plate of assorted cheeses and crackers; another plate stacked with beautifully carved cuts of chicken, steak, and pork. And that was before I even made it to the desserts, which were pushed in on their very own cart.

"The King and Queen weren't sure what you would like," said the man who brought everything.

That wasn't a surprise, but I was surprised by how much I ate. As soon as I saw the food, my stomach rumbled so loudly I thought it might shake the whole castle. I didn't want to eat alone, though, so I asked the man to see if Abbey could join me.

Not five minutes later, Abbey was seated with me and smiling as she choose a few pieces of meat for herself.

I'd finished my third plate of food when Abbey finally spoke. "When was the last time you ate?"

That jarred me—I'd gotten used to barely eating more

than a small child would. "I tend not to have much of an appetite, but I guess the journey here made me really hungry." I shrugged and changed the subject. "Could you tell me what this place was like before I got here?"

Abbey chuckled. "If you want to know the history of the castle, you need to know the history of Neville first." I simply nodded and popped another grape into my mouth. "Neville has always been a beautiful place with its fair share of different rulers," Abbey began. "All faced with their own challenges. Your father is the first King to have been the third in line when he took the throne."

"Why did he?"

"His eldest brother died suddenly in his sleep—his heart just gave out—and his next brother forfeited the Nevillian throne. He said there was a kingdom in greater need of a king elsewhere and we would be in good hands under your father's rule."

I picked up a different piece of cheese. "And people were okay with that? I don't know much about kingdoms, but that doesn't sound right."

"The King has a very strong relationship with his people," Abbey answered firmly. "He still does. And the hopes we hold for your father's rule are the same as the hopes we hold for yours."

I bit back a sarcastic comment and changed the topic. "Do you have any children?"

For the first time, Abbey hesitated before answering. "I did," she said slowly. "A very long time ago. But sickness traveled through my village. It was during the time when people believed that magic could only be used to heal the royal family of sickness." Her face lightened. "Until your great-grandfather decided differently, that is. He said that if the universe believed we were worthy of the gift of magic, then we should use it to benefit everyone." Her smile turned bittersweet. "It was too late for my son, only seven years, and my husband. They died before they could get help."

"I'm sorry."

Abbey shook her head and got up, stacking the empty plates onto the cart. "Don't be. We all have our paths that lead us to where we are. You know that better than anyone."

Judging from the wrinkles in her face, Abbey was definitely older than I was, but still, something wasn't adding up. "You don't look old enough to have been alive when my grandfather was, much less with a child who was only seven," I said doubtfully.

She chuckled. "Trust me, I'm very old."

I knew I should question that a little more, but a part of me didn't want to know. Instead, I asked, "Why didn't they have more kids? Isn't having lots of children one of the most important things royals can do?"

Abbey shrugged. "They couldn't. Whether they wanted to or not is a different question. I can't answer that, but I do know that some things you just can't control."

My eyes involuntarily narrowed. "What do you know about the prophecies?"

She only froze for a second before saying, "I'm a nanny. I don't know anything about prophecies."

I wasn't buying that. *She knows too much about me* not *to know about the prophecies.* "You're a much better liar than Tasar," I said drily.

She chuckled again as she picked up the last dish. "It's my job."

"I know they said something about the return of the princess," I said stubbornly. "And something about Hell walking Neville. I want to know what that means."

"Then you know who to ask." She pushed the cart back into the main chamber.

I let out a deep breath. I had no interest in talking to…*them.*

"Ready for bed?" Abbey asked me from inside my bedroom. "I'm going to start running your bath. You can put on a robe if that's more comfortable for you."

When I stepped inside the chamber, I saw a white silk robe lying on my bed. I picked it up and held the fabric close to my chest, feeling the smoothness of it on my skin.

* * *

CLAD IN MY NEW ROBE, I entered the white-tiled bathroom. A round bathtub stood in the center in the room. It was big enough for two or more people to sit in and so high that three steps circled the outside of it, leading up to the edge. Arched windows on one side of the room were covered with white curtains that billowed gently with the breeze. The toilet was out of sight from the windows against an adjacent wall, and two sinks topped with a large mirror stood against the opposite wall.

ABBEY WALKED OVER. "Let's take your hair down." She carefully undid my ponytail before I could answer. "You soak and I'll be back to wash you." She was out the door without another glance.

I UNTIED THE ROBE, letting it fall to the floor. The chill of the tile disappeared as soon as I stepped into the water, nudging aside the brightly colored petals scattered on the water. They were the same colors as the specks in the bar of soap sitting on the edge of the giant tub.

. . .

A STRONG GUST of wind came in through the arched windows, prompting me to slide deeper into the warm water. I could see the moon shining through the gauzy white curtains.

Then, suddenly, I saw something that made my stomach drop—a dark fog was creeping in from the balcony, flowing like water into the room. Part of me wanted to scream, to yell for help, but nothing came out. I didn't even try to shout —I just watched the fog circle my bath and waited for something to happen.

A chill ran up my spine despite the warm water. I turned and saw a figure sitting on the opposite edge of the tub with his back facing me. "Welcome home," he said.

I recognized his voice immediately—it was the voice from every shadowy nightmare I'd had. And I still didn't know his name.

"What are you doing here?" I asked, covering myself as best as I could.

Instead of answering, he asked, "How does it feel?" Thankfully, his gaze was fixed on the moon and not me.

"How does what feel?"

"Being home. I haven't been home in so long… I don't remember what it's like. Or what it will be like when I return."

"Where is your home?"

Silence. Which was somehow worse than him answering my questions with more questions.

"Do you smell that?" he suddenly asked.

I could only smell the flowers floating in the quickly chilling water. "I just smell the bath you're rudely interrupting."

He stood up from the tub, stepping towards the window as another gust of wind came in. "It's war. War is coming."

My vision frayed. I slipped farther down into the water, deep enough for it to cover my face. I hastily pushed myself up, trying to catch my breath, my heart racing.

The door opened and Abbey walked into the room. "Everything okay?" she asked with a slight frown on her face.

I looked around the room. There was no man, no fog—just me surrounded by floating flowers and moonlight. I looked at the gently waving curtains and shivered.

War is coming.

* * *

W*AR IS COMING.*

I laid in bed for hours, staring at the ceiling. A giant phoenix was painted on it. My body was relaxed, but my brain wasn't. And I knew that nothing was going to be able to slow down my thoughts.

With no sleep in sight, I tore the blanket off and stood up, feeling my long-sleeved nightgown flow all the way down to my feet. I went to my door and cracked it open, glancing up and down the length of the hallway. I didn't hear or see anybody.

F*ORTUNATELY,* enough moonlight spilled into the hallway to let me find Kit's room...or at least, what I was pretty sure was Kit's room.

I knocked his door, hoping it was the right one. No one answered. I had just turned to leave when the door opened. "You should be sleeping." Kit's voice said.

I turned back and saw him standing in the doorway with only a pair of pants on. Tattoos stretched across his chest. For the first time I could remember, his long hair was falling down his shoulders.

"So, you actually *do* let your hair down!" I spoke.

That got a small smirk from him as he ushered me into his bedroom. It was similar to mine in terms of the layout, but there was a lot more white and a lot less red.

"Your room is much calmer than mine," I told him as I walked over to the bed and perched on the edge of it. I let myself fall onto my back and looked up. There it was again! An identical phoenix arched across the ceiling. "Whose idea do you think it was to paint that? I have one in my room, too."

Kit likewise sprawled out on the bed. "It's a family crest. You kind of have to display that sort of thing."

"I didn't see one at your house."

"I'm not important."

I turned my head, looking over at him. "You are to me."

Kit chuckled. "You remember when we first met?"

"Are you kidding? Sure, I hit my head pretty often from all the passing out I used to do, but I remember. You called me a damsel in distress."

"You were." Kit finally looked at me. He smiled. "Or at least, I thought you were a damsel in distress. But I was wrong! You're very strong." He reached over and poked me. "And you haven't passed out even once since we've been here!"

I snorted. "I did—you just didn't see it." I let out a deep breath and directed my gaze back to the phoenix. "I saw myself in the mirror earlier tonight. I'm starting to look the way I used to! My skin still looks like I've never seen the sun before, but my hair has gotten its color back and my eyes are green again...for the most part." A tear slid from the corner of my eye. "But every time I look in the mirror, I see the red in my eyes. I can't make it go away."

I could feel Kit watching me. "Maybe that's not a bad thing."

"But what if it is?"

"What do you mean?"

His question made me pause. Hell on Neville, war... They each had a cause, and that cause seemed to be me. I would have been a fool not to notice. *This is my fault—it's not a coincidence that I showed up right before everything was on the verge of getting destroyed. I know that. But I don't know how to fix it...* "I don't know," I whispered, wiping my eyes. "I just don't know."

"You wanna know what I know?" Kit asked in a surprisingly gentle voice. I just nodded. "I know that you were thrown into a world you didn't know anything about. And you handled it. I know that you were given a truth you weren't prepared for. And you're doing the best you can. I know that you're going to be able to find your way through everything that follows. That's what I know."

I didn't want him to be wrong, but I didn't know if he was right, either, so I just let out a deep breath and kept my eyes on the phoenix.

* * *

THIS TIME, the hours of ceiling-staring were accompanied by Kit's snoring. I guess people sleep just great when they don't worry about attracting monsters with their dreams.

I slipped out of the bed and back into the empty hallway. I had nowhere to go this time, so I just let my feet guide me through the building. Eventually, I found myself outside.

It wasn't cold. The pleasant breeze seemed to calm my jangling nerves. I walked through the grass until I ended up by a pond with a bench next to it. The sound of crickets filled the night air. Something furry touched my hand, and I spun sharply around.

Axel sat staring at me. I smiled and rubbed the fur around

his ears as I sat down on the bench. "At least I don't have to be here alone!" He whined softly, still looking up at me. I could guess what he was thinking—I was thinking the same thing.

I'm screwed...and so is everyone else.

CHAPTER 14

I woke up to the feeling of someone watching me. Pain shot through my body as I pushed myself upright. *Sleeping on a stone bench has serious consequences,* I should have known that. When I looked up, instead of seeing Axel, my eyes ran up a long, fitted black dress all the way to Anna's black eyes. "Were the expensive beds not good enough?" Anna asked.

"I have problems with sleeping in an unfamiliar place," I said, trying to stretch away the pain in my limbs.

Anna chuckled. "Fear of vulnerability—you get that from your mother."

"Is that why she's so…intense?"

"Partly." Anna sat down on the bench next to me. "Fear is a very powerful motivator."

"Is that what motivates you?"

She gave me a slightly insulted look. "What do you mean?"

"You were going to kill me!" I said more sharply than I had meant to. "You didn't care what I had to say or what I was doing—you were going to kill me anyway."

She nodded and shrugged. "I like to think of it more as self-preservation. The King has a brother who's been dying to get his grimy hands on the throne! Has been since before my sister was even in the picture. Luckily, he hasn't stepped foot in this kingdom since before you went missing. My sister wouldn't allow it."

I frowned. "I thought he gave up the throne voluntarily…?"

She laughed. Despite it being a lighthearted sound, there was something unnerving about it. "No, he didn't have a choice! Everyone knew he wasn't fit for this kingdom, so he went off to find his own."

If the brother really wanted to rule Neville and he wasn't to be trusted, could that mean *he* was cause of all of this? "Does she think he had something to do with it? With me, I mean?" I asked.

"I don't know what my sister thinks."

"There you are!" Kit was walking across the grass, heading towards us. Anna stood up, a small smirk on her face, and walked away.

Kit stopped and watched her with suspicion before turning back to me. His expression softened. "Everyone was ready to send out a search party."

I sighed and got up. Kit immediately looked away from me and at the pond instead. He was good at not letting me read his face, but something was clearly amiss. "What's wrong?" I asked.

He glanced at me. "Nothing's wrong."

I walked over to him and lightly touched his hand. Kit let out a deep breath. "Why did you leave?"

"I couldn't sleep, so I went for a walk," I said with a shrug. "And I ended up here." I looked around for Axel but didn't see him. "Axel was here, too. Where did he go?"

"Back to the forest," Kit answered. "Most people don't

take kindly to being around animals that could kill them. Doesn't matter if they would or not."

He led me back into the castle and back to my room so that I could put some decent clothes on.

* * *

THE SECOND I stepped into the wardrobe, I saw Abbey standing there with two girls dressed in long black dresses and white aprons. "I'm Florence, Your Grace," said the girl who had her blonde hair done in a braid. She hastily curtsied.

The one with red hair refused to look up from her shoes. "I'm Mary-Anne." She spoke just above a whisper as she too curtsied.

"They're going to help you get dressed," Abbey told me. She turned back to the girls. "Make sure you clean her feet!" Her voice was stern when she addressed the girls but softer when she spoke again to me. "I'll be back to escort you to your lesson." Abbey left the room with a final look at the girls.

"I'll start the water!" Mary-Anne quickly said. She nearly ran into the bathroom.

An awkward silence fell, but when I looked at Florence, she was grinning at me. "What colors would you like to wear today?" she asked.

I took a deep breath. "You pick," I said. I headed towards the bathroom, but as I reached for the doorknob, I heard someone mumbling. I pressed my ear against the door.

"You're okay… She seems nice… Maybe…prophecy… problems… It's wrong… Maybe…no….truth… It's different… Something new…"

I opened the door. It was quiet inside. Mary-Anne quickly

stood up from where she had been bending over the tub, keeping her eyes glued to the floor.

"What were you talking about?" I asked.

"I don't know what you mean, Your Grace."

I knew she was lying. But how could I make someone tell me something they didn't want to tell me? My eyes got hot and my vision turned red. I shut my eyes, taking a deep breath.

"It's true." I heard Mary-Anne whisper. I opened my eyes. Thankfully, my vision was clear again.

"What's true?"

Mary-Anne just shook her head and looked down.

Rage started to boil inside of me. "I won't ask you again!" I spoke through gritted teeth in a way I never had before. I was surprised by how easily harshness seemed to come to me.

That made her look at me. I saw fear in her eyes. "I will tell you what frightens me, Your Grace, but I ask for your sympathy. I do not wish to dishearten or shame you. I do not wish to overstep my place. It's just…"

She took a deep breath, steadying herself. "I fear for the safety of my brother. He's one the King's servants. He helps the King with everything, and because of that, he has heard more things than a servant should. He knew he shouldn't speak about what he hears, but he couldn't keep it secret. I told him he could share with me and that I would hold his secrets. And I have! I have not told another soul! I promise, Your Grace."

My anger morphed into impatience. "Just tell me," I urged her.

Her voice fell to a near-whisper. "He overheard the King talking about the prophecies. The workers found four objects in the mines, not two. The King and Queen worry about your fate—and the fate of the kingdom—if they tell everyone about all four prophecies."

Curiosity made me tingle. "What are the other two? I only know about the princess returning and Hell walking on Nevell."

She gave a quick nod. "Those are what they let leak to the servants. Servants hear everything! If you give them nothing, they spread assumptions and eventually cause panic. So, your parents let them find out about the two prophecies."

I frowned. "But what are the other two?" I repeated.

She looked even more nervous. "Let me wash your feet. I'll explain then." She motioned for me to step into the tub.

I lifted the hem of my nightgown and stepped up into the tub, letting my grass-stained feet dangle in the warm water. Mary-Anne brought a sponge and soap to the side of the tub and began scrubbing my right foot.

"The tunnels under the castle were closed for years," she said quietly. "That was after Peter—he was the castle's crystal reader—started selling fortunes to whomever could pay him. Kingdoms were on the brink of war. Then you went missing. The Royal Majesties hoped they could find clues about your disappearance in the mines underneath the castle, so they sent ten miners to search. Only one came back."

Mary-Anne reached for my other foot. "But the remaining miner died at the entrance of the tunnel—he suffocated from the dust in the mine. Some people think he died of being cursed. That I do not know."

She looked up at me. "The first prophecy wasn't about the return of the missing princess, Your Grace—it was about the rightful heir ascending to the throne. No one knows if the prophecy speaks of an heir now or a future heir.

"The second prophecy did mention Hell on Neville, but it was about three plagues of darkness, destruction, and death. The third prophecy spoke of a break in the veil, which is what separates our world from the one of shadows. Then there was the final prophecy…" Mary-Anne trailed off.

"Keep going!" I demanded.

She finished rinsing my feet and sat back, her gaze on the water. "I don't know the details, but my brother said it had to do with you and uncontrollable power. A power that will destroy us all."

Fear ran through my entire body and made my knees go weak. I wanted to stand up, but I knew I would fall into the water.

Once I was able to stand, Mary-Anne carefully dried my feet and then fled. Florence poked her head into the bathroom and told me to come out to let her dress me. I dutifully obeyed, my mind swirling.

Florence buttoned me into a light blue dress. From the waist up, it fit snugly, but then it flowed downward, covering the silver heels she strapped onto my very clean feet. She braided my hair back and studded it with flowers.

By the time I walked out of my bedroom, Kit was standing in my doorway, leaning against the doorjamb. I couldn't stop smiling when I saw him. After all the bad news I'd heard about the prophecies, it felt good to be around someone comfortable. Kit was my calm in the storm.

"Don't you look like a royal?" he said teasingly.

I rolled my eyes. "As much as I would love to stand here and listen to you mock my pain, Abbey is coming to take me to a lesson."

"I thought *I* would escort you to your lesson. Got her to tell me the way." He extended his arm to me.

"How many jokes will I have to listen to along the way?" I asked, then took his proffered arm. We started walking down the hallway.

"I guess we'll have to see, Your Majesty."

I chuckled and let my gaze roam over the portraits

hanging on the walls. We went down the staircase, descending two floors, and then walked along another long hallway to a set of double doors.

"This is your stop," Kit said, lowering his arm. I let my hand fall back to my side. He opened the door and ushered me in.

"You aren't coming with me?" I asked.

Kit shook his head. "I've been asked to meet with the King." He tried to hide the nervousness in his voice. "But if you really need me to stay, I'm sure he'd understand."

I couldn't stop a smirk from spreading across my face. "Are you nervous?"

Kit scoffed. "I spend my time in the dark forest battling Hell Beasts! The King doesn't scare me."

A sudden idea occurred to me. "Well, then, who am I to interfere with your meeting? Have fun." I stepped through the doorway.

"You're not as funny as you think you are!" I heard behind me. I didn't have to turn around to know that he wore a smirk of his own.

I was in a library. Every wall was piled high with built-in bookshelves stuffed with books, and more stood in free-standing shelves. A path snaked through the room, its red marble floor bright against the light cream marble that disappeared underneath the shelves.

The path led to the center of the room before forking forward, left, and right. I followed the path to the center. A soft sound caught my attention—it sounded almost like a horse neighing.

I glanced around, but I couldn't find an obvious source of the sound. Then I heard a clicking by my feet. When I looked down, I saw something glinting. I bent down to get a better look. Despite not being able to clearly see what was creating the reflection, I held out my hands...

...and I jumped when a coldness leapt onto my fingers. I cupped my palms together and squinted. I was able to make out a glass figure of a tiny horse prancing in my hands.

"I've been waiting over twenty years to show you that!" a cheerful voice said. I looked up and saw the Queen stepping out from behind a bookcase. "Ever since I found out I was with child! I wanted to see your expression when you saw it."

"You have—" the word briefly stuck in my throat— "magic."

She shrugged. "That's just simple magic dust. It's a trick done at children's parties. But, yes, I have magic. Healer magic. It's rare, just like yours."

The horse in my hand laid down and turned into a solid glass statue. I could only gawk at it.

She grinned. "Come on!" I carefully set the crystal horse on a nearby bookshelf and followed her to a table laden with stacks of books.

I nearly gasped as I gazed up at the tall shelves surrounding us. "This is a lot!"

"Yes, and we have a lot to catch up on." She motioned for me to have a seat. "And you have a lot to learn."

Sitting at the table next to the Queen brought back memories of being in school and listening to the teacher ramble on and on, knowing I wasn't going to remember a thing when I got home. But I really tried this time—I tried to remember various regions on a map I'd never seen before, tried to memorize the use of different potions I'd never seen before, tried to stop slouching. Mostly, I tried to throttle back the curse words that wanted to explode out of my mouth.

"Where is the village of Dealthstone?" The Queen asked.

I stared at the blank map in front of me. I didn't know if she thought I had a photographic memory or if she expected me to just inherently *know* the map of the kingdom, but I did know that I'd lost every ounce of patience I possessed.

"I don't know!" I shouted. I slammed my fists on the table in frustration.

"There's no reason to shout," The Queen said sternly.

That only angered me more. "I'm not going to be able to learn all of this!" I yelled.

She stood up, her mouth set in a straight line. "Why don't you keep reading and see if you can find a better attitude?"

Before I could even say anything, she stormed away from me. Curses finally flew out of my mouth as I picked up the map and glared at it.

* * *

I SAT THERE for almost an hour before I heard steps on the path. A minute later, Anna appeared. She sat down and looked at me levelly. "Grace has you studying."

I sighed. "I thought I was done with school."

Anna chuckled. "Royalty is never done learning."

"I was hoping these lessons would help me control my… uh…magic." I still struggled to say the word. "But she has me learning about maps and potions!"

"None of these lessons will help you control your magic," Anna said bluntly. "You can read every book. Practice every day. Think about it every second. But your magic is a piece of you—it's like a mirror of who you are. And your magic is broken."

I was stunned by her casualness. "Wow! Tell me what you really think."

Anna shrugged her shoulders. "It's also not as bad as you think."

"Why are you telling me this?"

"Because Grace thinks that she can throw you right back

into the world you were born in and that everything will just work out somehow, but she's wrong. No matter how hard she pushes you or how hard you try, you'll never be a part of this kingdom. And you'll never be the ruler it needs."

I swallowed hard. *She's probably right...*

"I'm telling you this because I'm going to give you the choice they won't."

"What's that?"

Anna gave me a small smile. "I'm going to help you get home."

CHAPTER 15

I'm going to help you get home.
I'm going to help you get home.
I'm going to help you get home.

I COULDN'T THINK about anything else. Not about Kit and his very vague explanation of his meeting with the King. Not about Abbey and her lecture about the importance of education. All I could think about was going home. Sure, I would be alone again, but I was good at being alone. I only knew how to *be* alone.

There was one big problem. I knew that no matter what Anna said, the King and Queen would never let me go back. So, if I did try to leave, I would have to do so secretly.

Then there was Kit. He knew I was hoping to go home, but was he still going to support the idea? What would happen to him if he knew I was leaving and didn't tell anybody about it? *I can't make him deal with that on his own, that I knew for sure.*

It was too much to think about. The pressure was too much to handle.

I pulled my blanket over my head, hoping to hide myself from the world.

* * *

I DIDN'T FEEL like I'd slept, but when Abbey walked into my bedroom, I knew it was morning—she came every morning with tea and news of the day. My entire body started to shake under the large comforter; I stifled the curses fighting to leave my lips. She pulled away the blankets.

I wanted to pull the blankets back up, but my arms were too heavy to move. I just laid there with my eyes shut, paralyzed. I could sense the worry coming from Abbey. She covered me back up before leaving the room.

My teeth chattered. It had been so long since I'd been like this that my body had forgotten how to handle it. *Is it shutting down?* I wondered desperately. *Maybe I'll be dead before I even get a chance to go home...*

Then a warmth moved in my toes. Slowly, inch by inch, it rose, covering my entire body. My shaking quieted and a tenderness took over.

Peace took over.

* * *

I WAS NO LONGER in bed—I was lying in a field of grass under what felt like a bright sun. I slowly opened my hand, letting blades of grass weave themselves between my fingers. Their slight sharpness gave me the permission I needed to open my eyes.

The sun's rays blinded me as I easily pushed myself up. After my eyes had adjusted, I was able to see the beautiful flowers surrounding me: red, white, yellow, and light purple petals were scattered throughout the green carpet, making me smile.

I stood, feeling softness under my toes. A presence behind me drew my attention. A woman kneeled in the grass, her palms flat on the ground. Her head hung down and her vibrant red hair covered her face. The red dress she was wearing was ripped down the sides and at the hemline.

I stepped closer and reached to touch her shoulder. She threw her head back and her red eyes—my eyes—stared at mine. Fear shot through me. She reached up and gripped my hand so tightly that my knees started to shake.

"Don't let it happen!" Her voice was stern, strong, commanding. Like it didn't belong to me.

* * *

I WAS BACK in bed in an instant, gasping and trying to catch my breath. Warm hands on my shoulders were pressing me into the bed. "Don't move," I heard Kit's voice say. I started to relax.

"You scared us for a minute." That was Tasar. I looked over to see him standing on the other side of the bed with a bottle in his hand.

"What happened?" Kit asked as he sat down on the bed.

"Nothing! I felt great, so I took advantage of that. But now I can't even get out of bed."

Kit touched my hand, distracting me from my disappointment.

"I might have an answer for that," Tasar said. "When you stop breathing—"

I gasped. "I stopped breathing??"

"That's not important," Tasar said in a shockingly casual tone. I wanted to argue, but Kit squeezed my hand, and I pressed my lips together. "When you stopped breathing, a flux was created in the kingdom's magic. Magic is woven throughout every inch of the kingdom, so if the magic is interrupted, the world around us dies."

"What does that mean?" I asked.

"It means that someone or something is linking you to Neville. If they can't kill you separately, they'll destroy everything around you to do it."

"What does *that* mean?!" I nearly shouted.

"I don't know." Tasar turned over the bottle in his hand, frowning. "This magic—I've never seen it before. No one has seen it before. Or at least, no one is talking about it."

I felt like I was paralyzed again; I had to force myself to breathe. "Am I going to die?" I finally asked.

Tasar shrugged. "We all die eventually." He tried to hide his pity with a playful smile, but I could still see it in his brown eyes. He sighed. "But yes, you will die if we can't destroy the link."

"How do we do that?" Kit asked.

"For once, I have no idea." Tasar plucked a glass from a nearby table and filled it with dark blue liquid from the bottle he was holding. He handed it to me. "Although I do know that this will help slow the process. It's going to be a struggle to get down, but you don't really have a choice."

I took the glass, staring at the liquid for a few seconds before I tipped my head back and poured it down my throat like it was a shot. The second it hit my tongue, it started to burn. I drank fast, trying my best not to let it come back up.

After I finished the drink, I started to cough. And cough and cough and cough. An uncontrollable cough that seemed like it would never go away. I put my hand on my chest, trying to control my breathing.

Finally, the violent coughing ceased, leaving me with a sore throat. "I told you it was going to be a struggle," Tasar said. I just glared at him in response.

He chuckled. "You and the Queen have the same shut-up look." He gathered his things and left.

* * *

I SPENT all day in bed. Kit stayed with me until Abbey kicked him out, saying something about how a man being alone with a princess for so long was inappropriate. I rolled my eyes so hard I thought they might fall out of my head. Then I fell asleep without realizing it, only waking when Abbey checked on me and told me that the Queen wanted to see me. I reluctantly agreed that she could come in.

When the Queen walked into the room, she looked like she was ready to stroll down the runway—her blonde hair was pulled up into an elaborate bun underneath her crown and she wore a long pink dress with trails of red flowers winding down the sides.

She stopped at the foot of my bed. "How are you feeling?"

"I've been better."

She looked worried.

"It's happened before—I'll be fine," I said in what I hoped was a reassuring tone.

She nodded slightly. "How many times before has this happened?"

"More than I can count. It's a miracle that I can function at all."

She still looked troubled. "It makes sense that your hair and eyes were so faded and pale when you first got here," she said as she sat on the side of the bed. "They say we're supposed to represent the magic we have inside, and obviously your core magic was drained. But when your skin is also so pale, well..." She hesitated. "That's a sign of your spiritual pain. Of your soul crossing the veil."

I thought I knew what she meant, but I had to ask. "What's the veil?"

"It separates the undead from the living."

Even though that's what I had anticipated her saying, my breath caught in my throat. "And the place of the undead is like Hell…"

She nodded. "Except worse, because if you don't find peace, you end up stuck there forever." She reached out and lightly stroked my cheek. "But we won't let anything happen to you! You should talk to your father—he's been through this."

I wanted to ask her about it, but I didn't. I couldn't stop thinking about Hell.

* * *

THE QUEEN LEFT when I complained of feeling dizzy and fatigued. I was relieved to finally be alone, but by the time I was comfortable enough to close my eyes, it was nighttime. I was surrounded by darkness. I desperately wanted it to be a peaceful kind of darkness, but it wasn't. Still, I managed to fall asleep anyway…until an intense feeling ran through my body, screaming "WAKE UP!"

I shot upright, staring so hard into the darkness that my eyes hurt. Two eyes were staring back at me. I couldn't make anything out else until my eyes had adjusted to the faint moonlight coming through the curtains.

Kit was standing there. Black veins pulsed in his neck and trailed down his arms. It was unnerving, to say the least. "Kit, what are you doing? And what happened to you?"

His gaze was harsh and angry. *Something is wrong!* I thought as I shrank back from him.

He stepped closer. "I can't stop it," he hissed through clenched teeth.

"Stop what?" I hastily scooted to the edge of the bed, preparing to run.

Moving awkwardly, Kit gripped my shoulders and shoved me back down. A knife flashed in his hand.

"Kit, stop it!" I shouted.

"I can't!" he shouted back. Even though I could hear the struggle in his voice, his hard gaze stayed locked on me. I desperately grabbed his wrists and tried to push him away, ignoring my rising terror.

Despite my efforts, the knife moved closer towards my throat. Its tip glinted in the moonlight and my arms started to shake.

Then everything turned red, and I was flooded with a warm sensation. My ears started ringing. A scream erupted from me as Kit was thrown backwards, hitting the wall and knocking over a huge potted plant.

My feet touched the cold floor. All I could think about was death. *But I don't want to kill Kit!* I insisted to myself. I stood over him, my heart racing. Something caught the corner of my eye, distracting me. I looked down at my hands and saw a glowing red mist surrounding them.

The mist was moving restlessly. It wanted me to use it, I knew. It wanted to take down this entire castle if it could. It called for destruction at any means, destruction at any cost. *My* survival was all that mattered.

I looked back at Kit. He was sprawled against the wall, unconscious.

I squeezed my hands into tight fists, fighting the urge inside of me. *I won't hurt him. I can't!*

My breath deepened as I focused on breathing in and out, in and out. Slowly, my sight returned, and the mist dissipated.

The door swung open, and guards ran in. "You're a little late," I told them with a newfound sharpness.

CHAPTER 16

Guards picked up Kit and dragged him out of my bedroom. I tried to follow, but one of them stopped me. I remembered him—he'd been there when the guards had come for me at Tobyn's house. *Jedediah. His name is Jedediah...*

"You must stay here! We will tell your parents what happened," Jedediah said firmly. He gave me a brief bow and then shut the door behind him.

But I wasn't about to be stuck in this room! I ransacked the wardrobe for a dress I could put on myself and found a light gray one with buttons I could do myself. I left my hair down, slipped on some shoes, and stepped out into the hallway.

I roamed the castle halls for a while before I spotted Jedediah talking to the King and Queen. "He should be put to death for this act of treason!" the Queen snapped.

Rage boiled inside of me. "He will *not*!" I snapped. That got their attention. Jedediah stepped aside.

"He tried to kill you," the King stated.

"Because something is wrong with him! He couldn't stop himself. We need to help him, not *kill* him."

Jedediah cut in. "With all due respect, you don't know how this kingdom works and the dangers it holds."

"So, you're saying that killing him instead of trying to help him is the better option?" I asked in a hard voice.

"Of course not," the King answered quickly. "We need to find out what happened. Still, his actions cannot be ignored."

I met the King's gaze levelly. "I would be dead without him."

"And for that we are grateful," the Queen said in a neutral tone. But I could see Kit's death in her eyes—she had already made up her mind. "However, as the King says, this behavior will not—*cannot*—be ignored just because he's your friend. He will be made an example of."

She stepped towards me. The power radiating off of her told me that she wanted me to back down, to lower my head in defeat. "Do you understand me?"

My rage grew as I took a step of my own. The ground underneath me shook. "If anyone touches him, you will never see me again!" I snapped. I knew I was matching her power with my own. "Do *you* understand *me?*"

"He will not be harmed!" The King's voice pulled us out of our standoff. He looked at Jedediah. "That's final."

Jedediah nodded and turned. He walked away, leaving us.

The Queen frowned at her husband. "Lucius!"

"Enough!" His tone left no room for dissent. She looked away.

The King gazed at me, his face softening. "You're right—we've gotten too complacent about getting rid of the symptoms rather than curing the disease. Right now, Kit is the best chance we have of finding out who's against us. If there's a way to save your friend, find it."

I nodded and then took my leave, heading the same way

Jedediah had. *Kit isn't going to be able to tell me any more now than he could when he attacked me,* I thought grimly. *There's only one person who can help.*

It wasn't easy to find Tasar. He'd left a note on his door saying he'd gone to the library, but the library was a maze. I threaded my way through quite a few bookshelves and finally found him standing on a tall ladder, flipping through a book.

"Tasar!" I shouted without thinking.

He jumped, dropping his book, and had to clutch the ladder to keep himself from following the book onto the floor.

"Sorry," I hastily said.

He regained his balance and looked down at me. "Are you trying to kill me?"

"I need your help," I said. I bent down and picked up his book.

Tasar started climbing down the ladder. "I can only assume this has to do with Kit being arrested."

I just looked at him, shocked.

He sighed. "The castle may be large, but news travels fast."

"They put him in a cell?"

Tasar nodded, taking the book from my hand. "He tried to kill you. That's what happens." He walked past me, heading for another shelf.

I followed him. "You have to help me! Kit wouldn't try to hurt me unless someone was making him do it…"

Tasar angled a look at me. "Or paying him to do it. You never know what people are capable of."

My memory jumped back to the black veins pulsing down his neck. "There was black in his veins," I blurted out. Tasar stopped so quickly that I almost ran into him. "I could see it through his skin."

Tasar looked at me with a carefully neutral expression. "Just his neck?"

"And his arms. But that's all I could see."

"Did he say anything?"

"That he couldn't stop. When he spoke, it sounded like it took everything he had to get the words out." I could almost see Tasar's mind whirling. "You know something!"

"Only one way to find out." Tasar tucked his book into a stack on the shelf in front of him. He started walking away. "Are you coming?"

I nearly ran after him.

* * *

I FOLLOWED Tasar down endless hallways and four flights of stairs. The lower we went, the darker it got. Tasar led me to a candlelit archway with two guards standing in front of it. They looked at Tasar and didn't budge, but then they saw me and stepped to the side.

Without a word, we walked through the archway and into a long corridor lined with cells on either side of us. The first four were empty, but Tasar stopped in front of the next one. The candles inside it had all been extinguished, leaving it almost pitch-dark.

I took a step towards it. "Kit?" I tentatively asked. Tasar pulled me back just before a pair of arms shot through the cell bars and two dark brown eyes stared at me. Black veins wove through the whites of his eyes. I gasped reflexively.

"Stay away!" Kit growled. Then he disappeared back into the darkness.

Tasar shook his head. "He blew out all the candles in his cell," he said in a worried tone. "Can you put him to sleep so that I can get a better look at him?"

I bit my lip. "I don't know how to do that."

"You did it before!"

"Sure, when he tried to kill me."

"But you didn't kill him—you gained enough control over yourself to just knock him out. Do that again."

I crossed my arms and glared at him. "You say that like it's easy."

He lifted his shoulders. "I'm saying it's the only choice we have."

He was right. I took a slow breath in, closing my eyes, and tried to focus on all the times I'd felt my power go out of control. Maybe I could grab those sensations and bring it out again.

* * *

The man pulled on my arm, but all I could feel was my heart pounding in my chest. Everything in my sight turned red as I grasped the neck of the bottle and swung it hard against his head. I watched him slump to the ground as if I were observing myself through someone else's eyes...

The knife came closer. My heart throbbed in my ears and my skin felt like it was on fire as I pushed with everything I had. He flew away from me and slammed against the wall. I felt a wave of panic rush through me. Screams swirled in the air, sending sharp pains through my body...

* * *

Something quivered inside of me as my body started to heat up and my heart started to pound. With shaking hands, I focused my energy and slowly lifted my hands. A loud crash filled my ears, distracting me. I opened my eyes to see the cell door ripped from the wall and lying on top of an unconscious Kit.

"What's going on down there?" one of the guards shouted from the archway.

"Relax! We have it all under control!" Tasar yelled back before looking at me with a raised eyebrow. "Next time, hold back a little."

I let out a deep breath. "Let's hope there's *not* a next time." We squatted, each gripping one side of the cell door, and then lifted it together and leaned it against the wall. It was *heavy*! I had to take a minute to catch my breath.

When I turned to face Kit, my stomach dropped. His skin had paled, making the black veins even more visible, and he had black bags under his eyes. He looked like he hadn't slept in days. Tasar crouched down next to him and examined the black lines tracing down his skin.

I swallowed hard. "Do you know what's wrong with him?"

Tasar nodded. "He was poisoned."

"With what?"

"With magic—shadow magic." Tasar stood slowly. "Shadow magic is the worst kind. It's believed to darken the user's soul, for one thing. Drive them into madness." He met my horrified gaze steadily. "But no one in the castle knows how to use it. No one teaches shadow magic anymore—everyone who used to practice it was wiped out."

My stomach wouldn't stop twisting. "Do you know how to cure him?"

Tasar shook his head. "I have theories, but they've never been tried before...until now, that is." He gave me a small nod of encouragement.

I felt a spark of hope. "What do we need?"

"Go back to my office and find the shelf containing my potions. They're clearly labeled. Grab every bottle that starts with an S. Meanwhile, I'm going to the library to find the old spell books."

"Great!" I turned to leave, but then a thought popped into my head—what would happen if Kit woke up? Would he fly into some kind of murderous rage? "What about him?" I tilted my chin at Kit, still sprawled out on the floor.

Tasar gave him an appraising look. "I think he'll be fine. Let's just move fast." We exchanged nods and then rushed for the stairs, going our separate ways once we'd reached the main floor.

I had almost reached Tasar's office when I heard a door being flung open. "Anna, *enough!*" someone yelled.

I recognized the Queen's voice and pushed myself into a nearby door nook. Something told me I didn't want them to see me.

"My husband made a choice to follow my daughter!" the Queen said angrily. "How can I expect her to honor her father's legacy if I don't give her the chance to do so?"

Anna laughed. "She's a child who spent all her life in another world. She knows nothing."

"And maybe that's a good thing! Seeing as all of us have been dishonoring our duties."

"You aren't fit to be queen," Anna said icily.

"I'm the queen they have!" Her loud voice made my body tense; I could feel the power in it. "It behooves you to remember that."

Sharp footsteps sounded on the stone floors. I waited a few seconds, then popped my head around the edge of the doorframe. The Queen was striding away from me, and Anna was facing her. I seized the opportunity to scoot into an adjoining hallway.

I made it to Tasar's office without further incident. As usual, the room was littered with bottles. I started reading labels as fast as I could, seeing names like "Blaze," "Silence," "Disabling," "Explosions," and even more terrifying ones. In an effort to create order out of chaos, I lined up every bottle on the desk and then set aside all of the ones marked with a word starting with an S. Finally, I was looking at seven bottles. Six held red, black, blue, and green liquids of varying shades and one was filled with black powder.

I quickly retraced my steps, hoping I wouldn't run into the Queen or anyone else. The guards silently stepped aside when I rushed towards the archway of Kit's cell.

The broken cell door was still propped up against the wall, but Kit was gone. I felt myself panic. "Tasar?" I called out.

"Next cell!" Tasar replied. I hastily went to the next one to see Kit lying on the floor in the center of it. Tasar was leaning against a wall and flipping through a book. He looked up at me. "I thought it was wise to move him into a cell that had a door I could close in case he woke up."

I nodded and exhaled slowly. "I got everything."

Tasar carefully shut the book and set it on the floor. "I need the dark red one."

I handed the bottle to him. Tasar nodded a thanks and then waved a hand at the cell door. "Stand back."

I complied. Tasar picked up a candle from one of the wall nooks and dripped a few drops of the red liquid onto the flame. It turned dark red and flamed higher.

Tasar knelt next to Kit and held the flame near his arm. The harsh scent of burning flesh filled the air, but Kit didn't move at all.

Tasar moved the flame away and sighed. "Well, that didn't work. He should have screamed at the very least."

My sense of panic wasn't abating. "What now?"

"The black powder." I nodded and got out that one. "We're going to make a circle around him with it," Tasar instructed. "It should suck the magic out of him. That is, if the magic hasn't rooted itself too deeply."

I waited anxiously as Tasar slowly poured the powder in a

circle around Kit. Surprisingly, when he handed the bottle back to me, only half of it was gone. "How did you draw that with only half of this?" I asked.

"Half of what makes magic so powerful is how much you believe in it," Tasar replied absentmindedly. He stared at the Kit in silence. I had no idea what he was looking for, but nothing was happening. Tasar mumbled and ran his hand over his face, clearly frustrated.

"What are we going to do now?" I asked.

Tasar let out a hissing breath. "We try the really painful option." He gave me a grim look. "If *that* doesn't work, we can't save him."

I tried to make my mind go blank. "Which bottle do you need?" I asked in what was hopefully a calm voice.

"All of them." Tasar pulled a white cloth from his pocket and poured a good dash of the black liquid on it, then did the same with the rest. Once again, Tasar knelt next to Kit, but this time, he held the cloth over Kit's mouth.

Kit's eyes shot open, but Tasar kept the cloth firmly over his mouth. Kit struggled wildly, except somehow his arms were pinned to the ground—he could only writhe against whatever was keeping him down. I had trouble breathing as I watched Kit flail.

It felt like an eternity passed before Tasar removed the cloth from Kit's mouth. Kit rolled to his side; a second later, black liquid gushed out of his mouth. He started coughing worse than I had when Tasar had given me one of his liquids.

"It's working," Tasar said in a relieved tone.

I didn't let myself feel hopeful until Kit was able to take a deep breath without immediately erupting into a coughing fit. "He's cured now?"

Tasar shook his head. "No. He's got a good twenty-four hours of throwing this stuff up. And he obviously can't stay here."

"What about his room?"

Another headshake. "No, that won't work—that's the first place they'll check."

"Then my room. If I say that no one can come in, they won't."

Tasar agreed, but we were still faced with the problem of getting Kit there.

I sighed. "They aren't going to let us take him out of here. And we can't carry him the whole way."

"I have an idea." Tasar walked out of the cell without another word. I frowned at him. *What is he thinking?*

"Maisey…"

Kit's weak voice yanked me out of my annoyance. I quickly crouched down next to him and put my hand on his back. "I'm right here," I said softly. I could feel heat radiating from him.

He shook his head. "I'm so sorry…" His voice shook.

I just rubbed his back in response. Tears stung the corners of my eyes. "It's all going to be okay," I whispered.

We sat together in silence for at least thirty minutes. Finally, Tasar came back with a large cart with a white cloth draped over the top. It looked like the pastry cart the servants had brought me earlier. "We aren't hungry," I said wearily.

Tasar gave me a half smile. "I told the guards that you wanted sweets, but actually we're going to somehow get him into this—" he glanced at Kit, who was curled up into a miserable ball—"and roll him to your room."

I looked at Tasar askance. "And we'll carry him up four flights of stairs while we're at it?"

"No, we'll take the servant ramp."

I almost snorted. "You couldn't have told me about the ramp before I went up and down those stairs multiple times?"

"The ramp takes longer," Tasar said simply. "But we can't let a single servant see him, because none of them can keep a secret."

I sighed and helped Tasar pull the cart into the cell. Kit couldn't help us lift him and picking him up wasn't exactly the easiest thing to do. We lifted various parts of him, grunting with the effort, and finally got him tucked firmly into the cart.

We pushed the cloth-covered cart out of the cell. I held my breath as we passed the guards—why would a princess be pushing a cart?—but they didn't say a word. Maybe their policy was to just not get involved with a royal's whims.

With Tasar pulling from the front, we rolled the cart to a door that opened into to a long empty hall. Its slanted floor led up to the next floor. The incline made it even harder to push the cart; I cursed the whole way up.

We didn't run into anyone until we were laboring up the third slanted hallway and nearly collided with a servant who stepped out of a side door carrying a tray. Neither Tasar nor I spoke, but I could hear Kit starting to cough again.

The servant glanced curiously at the cart, and Tasar started coughing as loudly as possible, drowning out Kit. "Are you okay?" the servant asked. Tasar just nodded.

"He's fine," I said hastily. "He just needs some air." The servant nodded and started walking away from us.

We kept going and eventually ended up at my bedroom door. We'd just pushed the cart inside when I heard someone clear their throat.

Anna was standing in front of the balcony doors. "What are you doing here?" I asked as Tasar shut the hallway door behind us.

"I could ask you the same thing." Anna wore a small smirk. "Trying to save your pet?"

"He's not a pet."

"That would be more believable if he didn't follow you around like a lost puppy."

I just rolled my eyes.

"Why?" she asked in a snide tone.

"Why what?"

"Why save him?"

"Because that's what you do for people who have been good to you."

Anna scoffed, shaking her head. "In my experience, no one does anything for nothing."

I nodded. "Mine, too. Until I met Kit. He didn't give up on me, and I'm not going to give up on him."

She tilted her head and looked at me for a minute, then walked across the room and stood at the hall doorway. "Careful, kid. Love is a dangerous game."

The words shot out of my mouth. "I don't love him."

"Keep telling yourself that, and you might survive us yet." With that, she opened the door and slipped out.

CHAPTER 17

Tasar and I kept an eye on Kit for hours. He laid in my bed simultaneously soaked with sweat and yelling about freezing to death, and his whole body was shaking so hard that I found myself taking his hand in mine. I kept a bucket on the floor by the bed for him to throw up into every half hour. It sounded horribly painful for him, but he clearly needed to get that awful liquid out of himself.

News of his disappearance spread quickly—about two hours later, guards arrived and wanted to search my room. I didn't let them. After a very pointed and ungraceful conversation, they left me alone.

Halfway through the second day, Kit was starting to sleep more and throw up a little less. Tasar and I sat on the couch listening to him rattle and wheeze. "How long do you think this is going to take?" I asked Tasar.

He was leaning back with his eyes closed. "I have no idea. The book says it's rare that someone survives the first twenty-four hours. After that, it's just a waiting game."

"But he'll survive?"

Tasar shrugged. "Maybe." He opened one eye and saw the panic on my face. "But his chances are good," he added.

Tasar was soon snoring lightly. I wasn't. I was pacing the room, I was taking care of Kit, I was constantly listening to his breathing. It rattled with every breath he took.

"What are you doing?" Kit's weak voice asked as I had my ear to his chest. I lifted my head and looked at his face. Sweat beaded his forehead and his eyes were squeezed shut.

"Listening to your breathing."

A tiny smirk fought its way onto Kit's lips. "Be careful! You sound worried."

"I am worried," I admitted. "I worry all the time. I've been worrying ever since I got here. I think if I worried any more, I might explode."

"I get it. I… You…" Kit paused, letting out a deep breath. I waited for him to continue, but he didn't. We just breathed together in silence.

* * *

DAWN CAME AGAIN. I knew I looked like someone who hadn't left her room in days. The only reason I'd taken a bath and changed my clothes was because Kit had vomited all over me.

Tasar checked Kit's temperature, his expression solemn.

"How's he doing?" I asked, breaking the hush in the room.

Tasar chewed his lip thoughtfully. "Still pretty high. But some of that might be normal for him."

I frowned. "What do you mean?"

"Elfin body temperatures run higher than normal." He nodded at Kit. "His mother is Elfin. Usually when someone is at least half, they have the ears." Tasar pointed to his own as an example. "It's rare not to have them." He walked back over to the couch and sat down. "You met his brother?"

"Yeah. Why?"

"Having siblings is also rare for elves." He started nervously bouncing a knee. "Elves used to be seen as fools and thieves; sometimes people even called us traitors. When your grandfather brought the first elf to his court, there was such an uproar that most of us locked ourselves away. Some elves even lopped off the tips of their ears."

I let out a hissing breath. "I'm sorry you went through all of that!"

He gave a quick nod. "I don't go through it anymore. One of the joys of working for the King and Queen is that they need me."

I wasn't quite sure what to say about that, but after a minute of silence, I finally asked, "Why only have one child?"

"Let's just say that he's not the only one with scars." Tasar abruptly stood up and walked out to the balcony.

I didn't want to push him, but I also wanted to know more about what Tasar was talking about, so I told a servant to bring me some history books. At least it gave me something to do. And I was tired of having to ask people to explain things that I apparently should have already known. Things I didn't know because someone had taken that chance away from me.

I didn't get a book that could answer anything about elves, but I got one on was. One book in particular had been written detailing every war Neville had ever engaged in: the cause, what happened during battle, the number of soldiers on each side, what hardships the kingdom faced, who won, lists of casualties. The book also included thorough accounts from individual soldiers who either wanted to talk about victories or learn from their own mistakes.

A knock sounded on my bedroom door. Tasar poked his head in from the balcony. "Someone knocked!" he whispered.

"I know! Answer it," I said in the same hushed tone.

"I can't answer it—I'm alone in the princess' room with a prisoner we kidnapped!"

"You are so dramatic!"

Tasar's eyes moved to the book in my hands. "What are you reading?"

"Focus!" I snapped at him. "And hide yourself!" With that, I wedged open the door, blocking the view of the inside of my room with my body.

The King was standing there. "What are you doing here?" I asked him.

He smiled at me. "I think Kit will be fine for a moment."

My eyes widened. *How does he know Kit is here?* I wondered wildly.

"You and I are more alike than you know," the King said gently.

I just nodded and stepped out of my bedroom, closing the door behind me. He offered me the crook of his arm. I let him walk me down the hallway.

We walked in silence for a while. "Grace told me she talked to you about the paleness of your skin," the King finally said.

I nodded, racking my brain for exactly what I had talked to the Queen about. "Something about my soul."

"Yes."

"She said it happened to you…"

"Yes." Silence fell over us again. Soon, we were in a part of the castle I didn't recognize. Fewer doors lined this hallway. We stopped in front of a set of red double doors.

"I hate to say this, but our history is filled with war," the King said soberly. "Some were just wars; others weren't. It's sad, but it's true. And there will be more wars." He gazed at me with a haunted expression. "One cannot rule while being afraid of war. I know that well after what happened the last time."

"What happened?"

"I died."

My mouth fell open as the King opened the double doors. I forced my jaw shut and stepped inside the room. The floor was black marble and so highly polished that it reflected the oversized paintings hanging on the red-painted walls. Portraits of two older men adorned the left wall, and a painting of a younger man and another of an older woman hung on the right. Directly in front of me, I saw a painting of the King with an empty space next to him. In front of each painting, a podium displayed something: a pocket watch, a floating bright purple crystal that was slowly spinning, a scroll with writing on it, a pile of books, a golden sword.

The room was larger than it really needed to be, making me wonder if people came here very often. "These are portraits of every reigning royal of our family and the object that represented their rule," the King explained.

I started walking along the walls and stopped in front of the King's podium. It held a golden sword. "You said you died?"

The King nodded. "Yes. I was stabbed straight through the heart with a golden sword. But I was lucky—your mother was there, and she was able to use her powers to slow down my death until doctors arrived to stitch me up. Of course, it wasn't fixed completely. You can pull back a soul from crossing over, but you can't ultimately stop it from crossing."

"And the sword represents your rule?"

The King's expression sharpened. "It changed me—changed how I rule and how I make decisions. That event set the kingdom on a new path."

"So... You changed because your soul crossed over. And my soul crossed over, too. Or..." I paused for a moment, thinking. I felt like I was missing something. "Do I not have a soul?" I didn't do a very good job of hiding my panic at the thought.

He gave a slight chuckled. "Yes, you have a soul. Every living thing has a soul. Ours is just…damaged."

I tried to keep desperation out of my voice and only partly succeeded. "What does that mean?"

"No one has ever been able to answer that for me, but *I* can feel the difference. For one thing, what used to trouble me no longer does." The King clasped his hands behind his back as he walked over to the painting of the young man. "My father told me I had lost some innocence, the innocence that comes with death only being an idea instead of a reality."

He looked back at me. "I don't tell you this to scare you, but to warn you. Your birthright is not easy—on the contrary, it requires great sacrifice. If you truly believe in your heart that you shouldn't sit on my throne, I will let you go. No matter how much I don't want to."

I narrowed my eyes at him. "And you're just trusting that I won't leave for my own selfish reasons?"

The King faintly smiled. "You've spent the last few days trying to save the friend who tried to kill you. I don't think you're as selfish as you wish to believe you are."

We stayed in that room for a few more minutes, and then he escorted me back to my bedroom. Someone being honest with me made me feel much better, like maybe I wasn't just being blown around in the winds of everyone else's chaos. "Thank you," I said once we were at my doorway. "Normally, every time I talk to someone, I feel like I don't ever get any real answers."

"Your mother is just trying to protect you," the King said gently. "I think she's having a hard time seeing you as a grown woman instead of a newborn baby."

I just nodded. I reached for the doorknob, but something was bothering me. "Can I ask you one more thing?" I asked.

"You can ask me anything."

"Anna. She's…uh…"

"Intense?"

I chuckled. "That's one word for it."

"She has a hard hand on the affairs she handles, but she has good intentions. She always has." He paused for a moment, his gaze sliding away from mine. A slight glimmer in his eyes showed me everything I needed to know.

"You love her."

He quickly looked back at me. "She's my wife's sister," he stated flatly. "How about tomorrow you and I have lunch?"

I bit my tongue and nodded. "I would like that," I told him.

With that, I slipped inside my room and shut the door. I leaned against it, feeling good. A good I hadn't felt in a long time. I was starting to understand things!

I'd been stepping on eggshells, trying to decide what I should do and figure out what I'd missed seeing. *I've been trying to prevent something horrible from happening, and now I think I know what to do: I need to get out of the way,* I realized. *Whatever that means.*

CHAPTER 18

The next morning Kit was awake and alert. Tasar took that as his opportunity to get some peace and quiet—he said something about "If I don't get a second to myself, my brain is going to explode." I was too happy to see Kit in one piece to care about Tasar's complaints.

Kit was sitting up with the blanket covering him and his back against my headboard. I sat in the center of my bed with my legs crossed. I hadn't stopped chattering since he'd started acting alive again.

"So you had a good time with your dad," Kit finally broke in.

I felt my body tense up. "The King and I had a good talk, yes."

"Maisey, you can't keep them at arm's length forever."

"I don't do that."

"Really? Because you don't even call them by their actual names."

And just like that, this conversation is over, I decided. Aloud, I asked, "Do you remember what happened to you?"

Kit let out a deep breath and looked away from me. He

wanted to have that conversation as much as I wanted to talk about the King and Queen. "Not much. I remember leaving your room, I remember checking on Axel in the woods, and then…it's just…flashes that I can't seem to put together."

Kit shifted uncomfortably, and I reached out to put my hand on his. He looked at my hand before his eyes flickered back up to mine.

"It's okay," I said. "We'll figure it out."

"How do you suggest we do that?"

I scooted closer to him. "Where I'm from, we have these things called crime shows. Investigators show viewers how they figured out who committed the crime." My comments were obviously confusing Kit, so I rushed on. "They always say that witnesses see or hear something that's seems insignificant, but it isn't. Something always leads investigators to the person who committed the crime."

Kit's expression cleared. "You think the King and Queen know something. Even if they don't know they know it."

I nodded. "I'm having lunch with the King tomorrow. If I ask the right questions, you and I will figure out something."

Kit looked uneasy. "When people ask questions about you, they end up dead."

I pushed myself up from the bed, smiling at him. "That's why I'll be subtle! Small talk, pleasantries, all of that…and then I'll pry and pry until I have the answers I need. As King Walter, Protector of the Ancient Temples said, 'Every word will be designed and every action will be calculated. It will not end until what's right is what is upheld.'" I turned away and started walking towards the bathroom.

"Have you been reading history books?" Kit asked a second before I shut the door.

* * *

THE NEXT MORNING, a letter was delivered to my room. It said I should meet the King in the dining area by the castle's southeastern exit. I had no idea where that was, but fortunately, the letter was accompanied by a map.

I dressed carefully and left my room, my eyes glued to the map. Suddenly, a piercingly strong scream dropped me to my knees. Every glass window shattered; shards came raining down onto me as I bent over, trying to shield my face with my hands.

The screaming stopped, but a loud ringing sound was still making my ears feel heavy. I let my hands fall from my ears and did my best to brush away glittering shards.

Clomping, heavy footsteps sounded behind me. Before I could even look up, pain spread through my head and then down into my body. Darkness swept over me.

* * *

I STARTED to shake as the sound of my own labored breathing slowly pulled me back into reality. My cheek was resting on hard stones. I lifted my head and was instantly ambushed by pain. When I touched my temple, wetness dripped between my fingers.

I looked at the stones underneath me and saw water glimmering as it moved its way through tiny cracks. I slowly pushed myself up. *My shoes are gone,* I thought hazily. *And I'm wet...* Every part of my body was screaming in pain and utter fear. A cold breeze wrapped itself around me, making me feel chilled to the bone.

My eyes started to adjust. I noticed a dark lake and had cautiously started to step towards it when a splash made me quickly jump back. My eyes searched the water, trying to find the source of the noise. Slowly, a head moved above the water. Its skin had a gray tint to it; two icy white eyes stared at me.

"Just don't step in the water," a voice behind me warned.

I jumped and spun around. Anna was standing there, her long black hair flowing down over the straps of her black dress. She wasn't wearing shoes, either.

"They can't get you if you aren't in the water." She had a smile on her face but hatred in her eyes. With a snap of her fingers, torches lit themselves, shining brightly against the cave walls.

"What is this place?"

Anna shrugged as she circled me like a shark. "It's a private place I created—a mountain inside of the dark forest. It's not much, but it gives me the best connection to the other side."

"Why are you doing this? Why am I here?"

She wore a triumphant expression. "You want my whole story? Now we have time for me to tell it. No one is going to find us here. They would have to enter the dark forest for that to happen."

My brain went back to the castle—the screaming, the shattered windows, the heavy footsteps… "What did you do?"

Anna smirked at me. "Nothing that you didn't make me do."

A force suddenly pinned my hands behind my back. I winced, unable to move them. My heart raced under her glare. "I didn't make you like this."

She glared at me. "Your father did! He acts like a good man, but he's no better than anyone else in that stupid palace. They're all liars!" She sneered. "He promised to marry *me* but then fell for my sister as soon as she got into his bed. My parents wished I wasn't even there until they thought I could get them a title, but the second they realized I couldn't, they tossed me aside!"

Her eyes held so much pain that I flinched. "I did everything for them!" she shrieked. "The universe betrayed me by giving Grace healing magic and me *nothing*!"

Her voice echoed through the empty cave. She took in the silence before turning away from me.

I finally spoke. "Tough childhood? Sorry if I'm not sympathetic."

Anna chuckled and walked towards the lake. Stones appeared, creating a path that led to an oversized throne in the lake's center. She reached it and sat. "I can understand that," she said in a milder tone. "I may have been cursed with parents who didn't care about me, but absolutely no one cared about you. Not the foster father who used you as target practice for his empty beer bottles. Not the foster brother who tried to imprison you in your bedroom."

I brought my chin up. "Yet *you're* the one still complaining you weren't loved enough."

Anna abruptly lifted her hand; a half-breath later, I was lifted up from the ground. She whipped me around, spinning me and slamming me into the cave walls before she brought me back to hover in front of her. "I'd be careful what you say to me."

I'd done my best not to scream while I was being bashed against rocks. Now I ignored every growing bruise and used my most commanding voice. "If the universe betrayed you, how do you have powers?"

Her eyes narrowed. "I said I wasn't *born* with powers. I didn't say I didn't know how to *get* them. You need to learn how to listen."

I could only shake my head. "I don't understand."

Anna laughed. "Of course, you don't, sweetie. I've been playing with your innate stupidity since the moment you were born. What I could never understand was how you kept getting out of it."

I resolutely ignored my deepening bruises. "What do you mean?"

She sighed. "I really have to spell this out for you…" She crooked her finger and pulled me closer, holding me suspended over the water. The stone path she'd made for herself disappeared.

"I would have loved to squeeze the life out of you, but *he* wants to know more. Since I couldn't force myself to kill you —the idea of suffocating a baby was harder to accept than I'd thought it would be—I sent you away. I sent you to somewhere with no magic, somewhere where your magic would kill you so that I didn't have to. You weren't supposed to come back!"

I looked down at the water underneath me and saw tentacles brushing the surface of it. I nearly gulped, but then quickly steadied my expression. "All of this and for what? People are dying! The dark forest is killing them!"

She gave a slight nod. "Okay, I admit I wasn't trying to become Queen of the Bones, but sometimes it's easier to destroy and rebuild than try to fix all of the screwups."

Now it was my turn to glare. "You have no right to this kingdom! A prince can break a marriage promise if the union threatens the future of the people!"

"Someone has been reading her history books." She snorted and crossed one leg over the other. "Your father is dead, you're missing—and *you'll* be dead, too, once I drop you into this lake—and my sister…" She raised an eyebrow. "Well, let's just say I've been manipulating her since you first disappeared. I'll do it again, and this time I'll include that pathetic puppy you're so in love with. Then I'll rip her heart out and no one will be able to stop me."

Dead?? The King is dead?? What has she done? Or is that a

calculated lie? No, she's a liar. She can't be telling the true. My heart raced as visions of what she would do—maybe already *had* done—to everyone flew through my mind. Their terrified screams were all I could hear; I could smell the blood and destruction in the air as she stoked her war. *Darkness will follow,* I thought desperately.

Anna just watched me, small smirk pulling at her lips.

My vision went red. A burst of force ran through me. Seconds later, a strong wind hit my back…and then I found myself rolling on dirt-covered ground. The lake was gone; Anna was gone. All I saw was a mountainside looming over me and trees massed at my back.

I scrambled to my feet. *When I was lost in the dark forest with Kit, it took us* days *to get out. I don't have days!* But I had no idea how Anna had gotten me here—all I could do was run away from the mountain as fast as my legs would take me.

I didn't know how far I'd gotten when my legs started to shake. I leaned against a tree, gasping and looking behind me to make sure I wasn't being followed. I tried to listen for footsteps, but I couldn't hear anything except my heart slamming in my chest.

Then, finally, I did hear something else. "Maisey!" someone called in the distance.

Is that Anna's voice? I don't think so… I focused on taking deep breaths and calming my heartbeats. Gradually, they grew quieter, and I could make out the sound of hoofbeats.

"Maisey!" This time I recognized the voice. *Kit!* I shoved myself away from the tree and ran, stumbling, towards the sound of his voice.

Kit broke into a clearing. He was astride a brown horse, but as soon as he saw me, he reined the horse to a halt, hurriedly dismounted, and rushed over to me.

I wrapped my arms around him, using his strong frame to

hold myself up. "How did you find me?" I gasped into his shoulder.

One of his hands moved to gently stroke my hair. "I didn't. As much as I'd like to take the credit, Cordelia found you."

I loosened my arms and took a half-step back, creating enough space between us to look up into Kit's eyes. A brief weakness flashed through me. "I'm scared."

Kit used his fingertips to brush an errant strand of hair out of my face. "What happened?"

"Anna did this. She wants to get back at her sister. She wants to burn everything to the ground and rebuild the kingdom herself." My words were clipped and angry.

Kit looked horrified. "How did you get away?"

I quickly shook my head, memories of my reddened vision coming back to me. "I don't know. I just started to think about all the chaos she was threatening, and…well, I'm pretty sure I pushed myself out of that mountain. I don't know how. When I found myself outside of it, I just ran."

Kit nodded. "We have to get back to the castle." He let his hand fall from my cheek and took a step towards the horse.

I didn't move. "What if the Queen doesn't believe me? We can't go back there."

His gaze was soft, with none of the impatience I'd seen before. "Maisey, you must trust me. If I thought they would hurt you, I wouldn't bring you back."

Every feeling of mistrust vanished when I looked at him. For the first time, I could *see* him. I could understand the effect he had on me. It was suddenly clear: I trusted him. Really trusted him. *Kit has looked after me. He has protected me. He's given me something I can't even remember having before. I've made some mistakes in my life, but this isn't one of them.*

I stepped closer to him and reached up, placing my hand on his cheek. His gaze never wavered. I pushed myself against him and pressed my lips against his. The touch of his lips sent chills down my body; the warmth of his skin and his scent made the dark forest disappear. There was only us: there was no war, there was no magic, there was no fear, and, most importantly, there was no Anna.

That feeling of security couldn't last forever, I knew in some small part of my mind, but it didn't feel like it was going to abruptly vanish, either.

As his hands dropped to my hips, cupping them, I opened my mouth to say something…but not a single word came out. My burst of adrenaline was gone. My vision clouded and then went black.

CHAPTER 19

*S*top it! *Stop it! Stop it! I have to wake up. I can't be doing this again!*

"But you are." His voice sent a shock through my body. It was nearby and far away at the same time, right behind me and right in front of me, surrounding me like a toxic wave.

Darkness slowly moved away, letting in blue skies and green grass. But it wasn't real. It wasn't even pretending to be real. There were no clouds in the sky, no sun with its bright rays. No flowers dotted the grass. There was no sense of serenity. It was as if my subconscious wanted to make sure I didn't get lost in this fantasy.

Let. Me. OUT!

My voice came out strong and stern, but it didn't come from *me*. I put my hand on my throat, working it and trying to make a noise. No sound came out. Instead, a chill ran up my arm as I realized that he was standing next to me. I slowly looked up at him, not wanting to fall prey to his intense gaze.

"Your world is fake. Mine is not." He looked behind me.

Reluctantly, I turned around and watched the green grass and blue sky turn into the stone walls of the castle.

An agonizing scream shattered the thick silence, making me jump. *I recognize that voice...* I walked down the empty hallway, hearing only the sound of my own footsteps.

I reached the end of the hallway and stood in front of the throne room. Through the open door, I could see the Queen kneeling and holding her husband in her arms. Blood stained her dress, and her face was obscured by her long blonde hair as it fell over her and the King. Cordelia was standing helplessly nearby.

When the Queen finally looked up, the anger and pain in her face made her unrecognizable. "Find my daughter and bring me my sister!" she said in a raw-edged voice.

A teardrop slid down my cheek. "Why are you showing me this? Is this even real?" My voice emerged this time, but it was shaky and weak.

He was still beside me. "It's real. And it's time for you to choose."

"Choose what?"

"To fight or to leave. Your aunt is planning to destroy everyone in this kingdom. Everyone will die. You can either take your rightful place and stop her, or you can run. Something I'm sure you've been considering since you got here."

I looked into his bright brown eyes. "How do you know all of this?"

A half-smile. "It's what I do."

I hate non-answers and half-truths! I shook my head and started to turn away from him.

"But I should warn you, Maisey." I stopped in my tracks. "It's not likely that you'll both make it out of this alive."

I wasn't shocked. I wasn't even scared. *Anna has already tried to kill me twice...* "I don't need to be told that."

* * *

I shot upright. A quick glance around told me that I was lying in my own bed.

Kit was sitting on the side of it. "You're a hard person to read," he said mildly. My mind immediately went to how his lips had felt against mine. And then to the darkness that had ruined it.

"I promise to be way less complicated when this is all over," I told him, hoping I wasn't lying to him. I pushed myself off the bed. Everything spun briefly and then steadied.

Kit looked worried. "You okay? Maybe you should lie back down."

I shook my head and wished I hadn't. "I can't—we have a war to prepare for, and I need answers." I left, politely declining Kit's offers of assistance, and made my way through the hallways to the room with the portraits on the walls.

The Queen was there, staring at the King's portrait. I struggled to find the right words, but there were none. "I'm sorry," was all I could say.

She turned towards me, and before I could say anything else, she wrapped her arms around me. She held on like I was going to disappear if she let go. "I don't know how I didn't see this coming," she whispered.

"Anna is your sister," I said flatly.

She nodded and drew back slightly, then put her hands on my cheeks and looked into my eyes. A second later, her gaze returned to the King's portrait. "My sister wasn't always like this," she said with a sigh. "She wanted to make a difference. To make our parents proud."

"But something happened?"

The Queen shrugged. "Your father. After he died and I

managed to save him, he saw the world differently. He didn't see Anna's fierceness as being…" she trailed off, struggling to find the right word. "As being useful. Instead, he saw her fierceness leading to wars and executions. So, he changed the deal with my parents."

"He married you and not her."

She let out a deep breath, slowly nodding. "She was upset, and I understood that, but then when she got engaged herself, I thought we were past it. I didn't think she would ever do something like this."

Her eyes glassed over with pain, but she wore it with elegance, not letting her expression show the chaos that was surely running through her mind. "But after her own husband died and she'd had no children, she came back to the castle. She hid it well, but I could see it in her eyes—that infinite, angry sadness. Eventually, as before, I thought she'd gotten past it. Now I know I was wrong. I wish I would have asked her how I could have helped. Not that it justifies what she's doing now, but…"

A short silence filled the room before I spoke again. "We have to stop her."

"And we will." She finally looked at me again. This time, she'd pushed back the sorrow in her eyes. "She is a traitor, and we are going to end this."

She glanced at the King's portrait one last time before she led me out of the room. I watched her stride along calmly and decisively. She wasn't a grieving widow; she was a Queen. Power radiated from her. There was no doubt and no fear because there was no room for either.

"Where are we going?" I asked. I didn't even try to hide how in awe I was of her.

"The war room."

* * *

THE WAR ROOM was one of the largest rooms I'd ever been in. Tall marble columns outlined its corners and an imposing chandelier hung in the center, positioned above a large round table. The table was mostly covered with a map of Neville and the surrounding kingdoms.

Jedediah, Cordelia, Kit, and two men I didn't recognize were standing around the table. The Queen quickly introduced me to those two. "Maisey, this is Simon Juste. He handles the kingdom's treasury and all things valuable."

Simon was a dark-skinned man with no hair on his head but a thick black beard on his face. A scar ran across his closed eyelids. He dressed in black and held a walking stick. He smiled and slightly bowed his head in my direction. I nodded back.

"And this is Doan. He's in charge of information." Thin and tall, Doan had blonde hair that cascaded down his shoulders. Unlike Simon, nothing about the way he dressed was simple—gold chains dangled from his neck and a red-and-gold cloak hung from his shoulders. He gave me a wide smile that showed off rows of perfectly white teeth that were set off by a single gold tooth. "Lovely to meet you, Princess." Doan said with a curtsy. I didn't trust myself to curtsy and instead nodded again.

The Queen swept us all with her gaze. "Thank you for being here. I'll get straight to the heart of the matter since we don't have much time: Anna plans on destroying the entire kingdom to get the power she wants. If we don't stop her now, we won't be able to stop her later. So, any ideas?" The Queen looked at each one of us in turn.

"Anna has never been a fool—she's going to have monsters guarding her, and she's going to be prepared for anything we do," Doan pointed out. He nodded at Jedediah. "She even has her soldiers from the castle passing along information about what moves you make, Jedediah."

Jedediah rolled his eyes. "They could never know our plans."

"Enough! We are not here to argue," the Queen said firmly. She looked at Cordelia. "What do you know?"

Cordelia pointed towards the mountains on the map. "The source of magic is coming from inside this mountain. Given the type of power and the magnitude of it, Anna has to be up there alone." She tapped her fingers on the table thoughtfully. "I tried to send in eyes, but it's warded. She did make sure *one* person could get through, though." Cordelia's eyes landed on me.

"She wants me to go there," I said. Cordelia nodded.

"You can't!" Kit broke in, making me look over at him. "If you go back, she'll be sure to kill you."

I thought of the bright brown eyes looking at me. *"It's not likely that you'll both make it out of this alive..."*

I drew a deep breath as I looked away from Kit and at the map instead. "I need a path to the mountain."

Kit didn't say anything, but I could feel his anger radiating outwards like a heat wave.

"The army and I will clear the way," Jedediah said with a nod.

Cordelia smiled reassuringly at me and reached for a small wooden box sitting next to the map. She carefully lifted the lid, letting us all see the large blue crystal inside. A small light moved within the crystal as if something was trapped inside of it.

She handed me the box. "If you drop this stone into the core source of the magic, it will destroy the magic, taking all of the shadow monsters with it and breaking the barrier around the mountain."

I hesitantly reached for the box. "How will I know where to put it?"

"You won't be able to miss it. Trust me."

As soon as my hands touched the box, I could feel the crystal pulsing. Somehow, it was making my powers shake deep inside of me.

* * *

EVERYONE LEFT to prepare for our journey into the forest the next day. Everyone, that is, but Kit and I.

With the box still in my hand, I walked over to the window. The sky was almost blotted out by a dark black cloud. Occasional streaks of lightning flashed through it.

"You know, when we first met, this is not how I imagined things would go," Kit said from behind me.

"Do you believe in destiny?" I asked without looking at him.

"I BELIEVE we control our own fates. We're too small and too insignificant to matter so much."

I turned around. Kit was only inches away from me. "Have you always been so cynical?"

"You aren't always a ball of positivity yourself," he pointed out.

I couldn't stop smiling, but it was a bitter smile. "I know you aren't happy about me going. When you get angry, that anger radiates from you, you know." Kit scoffed, looking down as I continued. "And I realize that I don't know how to fight. But I can't just wait here and do nothing!" I looked down, too. "I can't stop just because I'm scared," I said in a softer voice.

Kit reached out and took my hand. I looked up at him. "I haven't fought in a war, either," he said gently. "The last great war ended when I was too young to fight. That's why you and I are going to do this together."

"You can't follow me into that mountain!" I protested.

"Maybe not, but that doesn't mean I can't be your eyes."

Before I could say anything else, Kit gently tugged on my hand. I followed as he led me down the hall, taking us through one of the arched stone doorways and into a grass field.

Cordelia was already there, sitting cross-legged in the grass and wearing a blue silk robe. A ball of water slowly spun in the air in front of her.

"Your anxiety is blocking my connection," she said without even glancing at us.

Kit stepped in front of her. "We need your assistance."

The ball of water stopped moving and she looked up at him. "Take my pause as curiosity."

"We all know that Maisey is the only one Anna will let into the mountain, but there has to be a way to protect her from a distance." Kit smiled faintly. "I learned a long time ago there's a loophole in every spell."

Cordelia let the water dissipate and stood, her robe waving and shifting as though it were water itself. "And luckily for us, we know someone with the power to create something like that."

Turning, she smiled at me. "Let's see if we can give Anna a real fight."

CHAPTER 20

Cordelia had me change into a red robe, in the process saying that I had to hand over my shoes. I tried to ask why, but she didn't answer. It was as if she was too busy having a conversation in her head to worry about responding to me. I just followed obediently as she first took me to my wardrobe and then back into the field where we'd found her.

She tilted back her head and stared at the sky, soaking in the silence. I waited patiently, not wanting to interrupt her concentration.

"I want you to close your eyes," she finally said. She let her chin drop and turned to face me. "I said close them."

I gave her one more long look before I closed my eyes.

"Focus on your breathing," she told me. "Focus on the scents in the air and the way the grass feels on your skin."

The green blades pricked my feet, especially when I moved my toes, and the fresh, brisk air sent chills rippling through me.

Her voice came again. "You have to find your link."

I opened my eyes. "What?"

Cordelia sighed. "If we're going to use your magic to create the weapons we need, you need to be able to focus your magic."

I thought about blowing the door off of the cell Kit had been in. "I've done that before."

She gave a slight shake of her head. "There's a difference between *using* your magic with no control and being *connected* to your magic."

I sighed. "Do I have to remind you that I've never done this before?"

Her direct gaze was unsympathetic. "It's true that most people learn to do this when they're five, but that doesn't mean you can't learn now." She gestured at me, circling her hands. "Your magic is an integral part of you—it's like an arm or leg. If you have no control over it, it's only going to cause you problems. Finding your link will allow you to bind who you are with what's inside of you."

"What's your link?"

"Water," she said crisply. "I was born in a lake, or at least at the edge of one. Midwives often say that being in water eases the process of giving birth." Her eyes didn't betray any emotion. "My mother died during childbirth. The other women scrambled to save her, and in the confusion, I was nearly lost, too. I should have drowned, but my magic kept that from happening—it created a bubble of air for me to breathe and held me near the surface. That's what a link is: a connection."

I closed my eyes again, taking a deep breath. I focused on the chilly air going in and out of my lungs. I searched my mind for anything that could be my link, but all I saw was floating darkness. I opened one eye to see Cordelia staring at me. "How will I know when my connection is right?"

"You'll know."

That was completely unhelpful, I thought. At least I managed not to blurt it out.

I stood there for what felt like hours, trying to find any link, any connection. Nothing. I tried again and again to find that missing piece of myself, but the only thing I could think of was death and running away from it.

Finally, I gave up. A person can only stand for so long in the silence of their own memories.

Cordelia must have felt the disappointment that I knew was radiating from me in waves. "You go relax," she said finally. "I'm going to see if Tasar has something to calm your nerves."

I just nodded and watched her walk away, feeling defeated.

* * *

I WENT BACK to my room and changed out of the red robe and into a simple short-sleeved red dress. Feeling adrift, I walked aimlessly down several hallways, not paying attention to where I was going.

Which is how I ran straight into Doan. "Sorry, Princess!" he said as he dipped his head.

"No, I'm sorry! I should have watched where I was going."

Doan smiled. "This is your castle. Nothing has to be your fault."

I frowned. "That seems like a dangerous idea…"

"Maybe, but it could be fun." He gave me an assessing look. "A little bird told me you're having a hard time finding your link."

I crossed my arms. "Cordelia told you that."

"No."

"How else would you know?"

He gave me a sideways look. "It's my job. If information were power, I would be a very powerful man."

"That line..." A different voice made me quickly turn around to see Simon standing behind me. "Didn't work on me, and it's not going to work on her." Simon's sightless eyes turned to me. "Something is bothering you."

I hesitated.

"Don't bother lying—he can sense it," Doan half-whispered.

"I have good hearing as well," Simon said immediately.

I gave in. "We're trying to find a weapon I could use to get through the barrier Anna created, but we have to use my powers to find it...and that requires control I don't have," I admitted.

"Control isn't going to get you what you want," Doan said.

"He's right," Simon agreed.

I lifted my shoulders helplessly, looking from one man to the other. "I don't know what that means."

"Everything about you is against the odds," Doan explained. "You lived longer in the no-magic world than people thought you would, and your magic survived longer than anyone thought it would. And to be honest, most of us thought you would have run away crying by now." He ignored the insulted look I gave him.

"I didn't," Simon said with a hint of pride in his voice.

Doan smirked at Simon. "For a blind man, you're a show-off!" Doan's gaze resettled on me. "My point is that if you go around treating your magic like everyone else treats theirs, you won't get anywhere."

That didn't make me feel any less lost. "So, what do I do?"

"Stop listening to everyone else," Simon said.

I repressed a scoff. *As if that's the simplest thing I could do!*

Nothing has been simple since I got here. Since my entire sense of reality was flipped upside down.

But I had nothing to lose.

I nodded at both of them even though Simon couldn't see me. With that unspoken consent, Doan and Simon walked me to the weapons room. The chamber was cavernous, with various swords, axes, war hammers, and daggers hanging on the walls. Throwing stars, arrows, and knives were stacked neatly on a sturdy table. More weapons I didn't recognize were on racks.

Simon and Doan stood by the doorway as I looked around. "Remember, you want to start small," Simon instructed me. "Choose something that will give you an advantage but also something that Anna won't see coming."

I picked up one of the arrows and stared its point, then tried to find some clear space on the table. I set down the arrow and took a deep breath, holding my hands over it. I closed my eyes. *I don't know what to focus on, but maybe it will come to me. If this magic is part of me, maybe, just maybe, I'll find it. My missing limb, my core...*

Something started happening. My heart started to race; my hands started shaking; my body warmed into a bright heat. Waves of slow pain slowly moved through me.

Then, suddenly, bursts of pain flashed through my head, threatening to bring me to my knees. Red eyes bored into my mind. Flames shot up from cracks in the earth as screams tore through the darkness and dead bodies gathered in gory piles.

A woman emerged from the hellscape, stalking towards me, staring at me. She was glaring at me, capturing my gaze, not letting me look away...

I was staring at myself, at my own red hair and red eyes. The look on her face—*my* face?—wasn't just anger, it was something stronger. Something dangerous.

I gasped, struggling to find my breath. It took a great effort to force myself back to reality. I leaned against the table, trying to calm the storm of images cascading through my mind.

I heard someone else gasp. "I can't see much, but I can sense power!"

Simon's voice made look at the arrow still lying on the table. A red glow had enveloped its silver tip.

Gingerly, I picked up the arrow and squinted at it. I could see tiny symbols carved into the tip of the arrow. *Is that enough?* I wondered. I sighed. *It has to be—I can't do that again. This is all we have.*

* * *

HAVING some kind of weapon was better than not having anything, even if I had no idea what the symbols meant. But I still felt as if I had let someone down. Like I let *everyone* down, really. *I should have been able to do more,* I fretted.

Doan and Simon accompanied me back to my room. Kit was already there, waiting for me. I walked over to him and held out the arrow. "I made a weapon for you. If I tried to use it myself, I would probably hurt myself." I handed it to him.

"How did you do it?" he asked as he carefully turned it over in his hand.

"Just focused…somehow…doesn't matter. But I can't do it again."

He looked back up at me. "Fortunately, I'm a good shot." He reached into his pocket with his free hand and withdrew four little orange balls. "These are what will take us to the mountain," he said.

I bent forward to scrutinize the orange balls. "You think of where you want to go, and it opens a portal to go through," he explained. "It's how I got to you so fast when

Cordelia found you after you'd gotten away from Anna." He nodded down at the balls, placing two in one of my hands. "Two of these will get us through from the castle to the mountain, and you'll take the other two with you. Then you'll have one to bring you into the mountain and one to bring you back to me. I figured you don't know how to rock climb."

Tears pricked the corners of my eyes. "But I still have to stay alive long enough to fix all of this." I looked out the window at the darkening clouds. They had moved closer.

Kit took a step towards me; now he was only inches away. "I put the word out. People are coming to help. We are going to win this war."

"And then what?" I snapped. "What happens when it's over?"

"We'll figure it out." Kit cupped my cheeks, turning my face to his. "Together." His thumbs caressed my cheeks.

I murmured "together" and leaned into his touch.

A loud thunderclap sounded in the distance, startling us. We both looked out the window just as the black clouds were cleaved by white lightning.

Kit sighed and moved his hands down to my arms. "It's time."

CHAPTER 21

Everything started moving so fast, with soldiers running down the halls and servants running into the cellars to hide until it was over.

The only servant not running for safety was Abbey. She pulled me into the wardrobe. "You can't fight in a dress," she told me. I felt my heart jump with happiness. It had been so long since I'd worn pants! They were black and loose-fitting and had one engraved button at the waist.

Abbey tucked the bottoms of the pants into a tall pair of black boots and then buttoned me into a thick woolen shirt. She took a step back and looked at me with tears in her eyes. "You make it back here!"

All I could do was nod and hurry out of the room. When I got to the main castle gates, I found everyone waiting for me. Kit stood next to a white-and-gray horse with a bow in his hand, arrows on his back, and a sword on his hip.

The Queen walked over to me. She was also clad in black pants and wore her blonde hair in a braid. The sword hanging at her hip drew my eye. I looked more closely and saw that the hilt bore her name spelled out in tiny red jewels. "Have you been in a fight before?" I asked.

The Queen smiled at me. "Your father wanted me to be prepared just in case I had to lead his army. Now it's your turn: you need to get into the mountain and sever the source as fast as you can. Once you've done that, Anna's barrier should dissipate, and we'll be able to get you out."

I nodded. She hesitated and looked at me for a moment before walking away towards the front of the line. Kit mounted and then held his hand out to me. I grasped it and swung into the saddle behind him.

Soldiers pulled open the heavy gates and we rode through. My mouth dropped when I took in the scene from behind Kit's shoulder: buildings and homes had been torn apart, flames were consuming what was left, and bodies were stacked atop more bodies. Men, women, even children—no one was safe from the destruction.

Cries split the air. Suddenly, something screeched above the tumult, something that sounded like a monstrous sort of battle cry. Kit spurred his horse forward. I buried my face in his back as we charged through the crowd, doing my best to ignore the screams until they became distant echoes behind us. The horse's hooves thudding into the ground were drumbeats that rattled my bones.

Finally, the horse slowed. I unclenched my hands from Kit's waist and looked up to see the edge of the dark forest. A mountain loomed over us. As soon as Kit reined the horse to a halt, I took a deep breath and forced my muscles to obey my brain's command to dismount.

Kit swung from the saddle a second after I did. "Breathe," he said.

I wrenched my gaze from the mountain and turned to look at him. "I'll breathe when this is over."

"I'm going to be there for you," he reminded me as he

tapped the bow slung across his chest. "But I need to get the right vantage point first."

I shook my head. "We can't kill her."

"Yes, we can. If we don't, she'll kill *you*."

I gave him another stubborn headshake. "The Queen needs answers! Just give me some time to try to talk to her. Anna isn't stupid."

Kit paused, clenching his jaw. "Fine," he finally choked out. "But if she tries to kill you and I have the shot, I'm taking it."

I pulled one of the small orange balls out of my pocket. Then I glanced back at the top of the mountain. A beam of purple light shot up into the darkening skies; it was obviously fueling the ominously massing dark clouds. *That's where I want to be.*

I tossed the ball onto the ground. A circle big enough for me to step through sprang up into the air. With a final look at Kit, I took a firm step into the circle…and found myself on the mountain's flattened peak.

I didn't see Anna or anyone else—it was just me and the purple beam. I reached into my pocket and wrapped my fingers around the crystal Cordelia had given me as I carefully approached the light emanating from a big jagged hole in the ground.

Then, before I could take another step, a strong force slammed me into the ground. Pain radiated through me. "I knew that was too easy!" I muttered. Grunting, I got back up. I touched my temple and felt wetness dripping down towards my eye.

"You shouldn't have come up here," I heard from behind me. I turned and saw Anna standing a few paces away.

"So then why did you make sure that I was the only one who *could* come here?"

She shrugged. "I didn't think you were that stupid."

I raised my hands in surrender and started to slowly walk towards her. "I just want to talk."

Her eyes narrowed. "Go on."

I took a deep breath. *This is going to be the most important speech of my life...* "Watching so many people die can't be what you wanted," I said evenly. "You killed someone you cared about, and you betrayed your sister."

"My sister betrayed *me!*" Anna snapped. Her voice was heavy with grief.

"And that's why you're going to keep killing everyone?"

"Yes." A smirk spread across her face as she stepped closer to me. "I knew you'd come here—I knew you'd either try to talk to me or distract me or just plain kill me. And unlike you, I know magic. I linked myself with the man you love."

At that, my heart started racing. Her smirk became a cruel grin. "You kill me, and he dies."

I lost it. Without even registering what I was doing, I launched myself at her and punched her as hard as I could in the face.

I didn't have time to land another punch before she slammed me into the ground again with another wave of force. "You thought you could beat me? You don't even know how to use magic!" Anna laughed.

Now she lifted me into the air; I could only helplessly watch my feet drift farther from the rocky ground as she cackled at me, purple light rippling outward from uplifted her hand.

"You're a child! You can't rule this kingdom! You're broken!" She threw me back onto the ground. I barely managed to fling up my arms in time to avoid smashing my head into a rock.

I lifted my head and saw the purple beam shooting out of the rock only a few paces away from where I was lying. I glared at her. "I didn't come here because I thought I could beat you."

She sneered and strode towards me. "You are a stupid, stupid girl."

I could feel the heat of the beam. I reached a furtive hand into my pocket and palmed the crystal. "I wasn't stupid enough to think that I could beat you," I told her a second before I rolled to my side and threw the crystal into the jagged hole. Quickly, I shoved myself backwards as the beam got brighter and hotter. My skin felt like it was about to broil itself off of my bones.

Suddenly, the purple light snuffed itself out. A thick silence descended on the mountaintop, shattered a second later by Anna's scream. *"What did you do??"*

It was my turn to sneer at her. "I knew I couldn't beat you, but I knew you couldn't resist showing me that *you* could beat *me*. And I knew that would give me the opportunity I needed." Slowly, achingly, I got to my feet, stumbling before I finally regained my balance. The black clouds above us started to lighten.

A tear rolled down Anna's cheeks. "I gave up everything for this," she whispered. She glared at me with more hate than I'd ever seen in anyone's eyes. "You have no idea what you've done!"

The air grew heavy. A dark mist coalesced around us, swirling in a circle. A buzzing sound erupted from it; at first, it sounded like gently humming bees, but then it got louder and louder, increasing in harshness until it made me think of a horde of angry hornets.

I clapped my hands over my ears and was about to flee when the mist moved away from me, shifting to envelop only Anna. It thickened, obscuring her to the point where I couldn't make out her face—I could only hear her scream.

The mist shifted again, shaping itself into a vague figure.

A hand reached out from it and entered the blurred outline of Anna. She briefly came into focus again, just enough for me to see the hand reach into her chest and pull out her beating heart.

Then the figure disappeared, leaving Anna and her heart to fall to the ground.

I stared at her. I'm not sure what I was waiting for, but nothing came. Only silence reigned. Only my breath existed inside that silence.

Her words floated through my mind: *"I linked myself with the man you love..."*

Panic filled me. I shoved my hand into my pocket and found the orange ball. With shaky hands, I pulled it out and created another doorway. I rushed through...and found myself back at the base of the mountain.

"Kit!" I shouted, frantically scanning the tall trees around me. *Think!! Where would he be? He was trying to find a good vantage point—what seems like a likely spot?*

I heard a groan, and then another. I followed it, my ears straining, and found him lying underneath a tree with his weapons scattered around him. Broken tree branches and torn leaves attested to his fall.

I dropped to my knees next to him, his breathing rasping in my ears. I could only imagine what he might have broken. "Kit, you're going to be okay," I said. "Look at me, please!"

He opened his eyes and tried to focus, but his brown eyes struggled to find me. I gently cupped his cheeks with my hands, tilting his gaze towards me.

His lips parted and he struggled to speak. "Maisey..."

I wanted to run and get help, but I couldn't leave him alone. "Just hold on!" I begged him. His eyelids started to flutter. "No, Kit! You promised to be here for me. You can't leave yet! We haven't had enough time!"

Kit reached out blindly, fumbling for my hand. I clasped it with one of my mine, still stroking his cheek with the other.

For the first time since I'd known him, I saw tears forming in his eyes. "I... I..." He took a deep breath. "I—I love you." A final breath escaped from his lips.

I froze as I watched the light in his eyes slowly dim. I laid a hand on his chest, searching for a heartbeat. A waterfall of tears welled up behind my eyes and my chest tightened, making it impossible to breathe. My blood started to boil in the deepest depths of my being.

Cries ripped out of me, turning into screams that shattered the cold air. My magic shot out of me like daggers, daggers that were now bloody with the pain of my reality.

I didn't say goodbye...

I never get to say goodbye...

EPILOGUE

$\mathcal{N}$ighttime in the castle. Only silence greeted me as I wandered the stone hallways, my long red nightgown keeping the cold at bay.

That was when I heard it: the voice I had battled with before. The voice that had continued to visit me every night since Kit had died. I followed the voice through the hallways and into the garden. The full moon shone down from a clear night sky.

That's when I felt *him*. He was standing right next to me, but I didn't have to look at him to know that. I had the same feeling I'd had every other time he had appeared: the shiver that twined itself along my spine. My powers reacted to him in a way that I didn't understand. They stirred inside of me like they were trying to tell me something, but I didn't have the time or energy to care what the message might be.

He'd said I would need his help. I didn't know if things could have turned out differently with his help, but I wondered. Somehow, I knew he was coming for a reason—he wanted something—and I knew there was going to be a cost to be paid.

But can he give me what I want?

"He's waiting for you." His voice was deep and strong, matching the energy that always radiated from him. "With my help, I can make sure you get everything you want." A large pale hand appeared in front of me, its palm facing up and waiting. "Come to him, Princess."

I stared at his hand. *Am I willing to take this step? I don't know if he's telling me everything, but I know what I want. I know what I need.*

I knew that I could be about to make the biggest mistake of my life, that listening to him could lead to unfathomable consequences. *But I just can't escape the feeling that this power that comes from him... Maybe he* could *be telling the truth. Maybe he* could *give me what I want.*

I slowly placed my hand in his and let him lead me through the castle. We passed through hallways I'd never seen before and went up a back stairwell that wrapped around one of the castle towers. A single wooden door perched at the top. He opened it, but there was nothing in the room except for dust and a small window.

He walked over to one of the walls and waved his hand in front of it. A black door appeared. Gold snakes undulated around the edges of it, their scales gleaming in the moon-light. He swung open the door and ushered me into a very different room.

This chamber looked nothing like the neglected antechamber—a plush black rug sprawled across the polished wood floors and an elegant bookcase traveled up one of the walls. But none of that caught my attention. What did draw my eyes was the red chair sitting next to the fire-place. A slim woman was sitting in the chair, a baggy black dress covering her frame and even darker hair falling over her face.

"She's going to help us both get what we want," he said, walking closer to the woman.

"Who is that?" I finally asked.

He towered over her for moment, then reached out and lightly touched her shoulder. "Say hello to your niece, darling."

The woman's chin slowly came up. Her hair fell away from her face, letting me see features that made my heart stop and my blood boil.

Anna.

ABOUT THE AUTHOR

Lizzy Richmond has been in love with writing for as long as she can remember. It's a part of who she is and sharing her stories have been a dream she couldn't be happier in sharing her work with the world. She lives in Michigan where her family has lived all her life.

When she's not writing or reading, she's cooking meals for her family or playing with her loving dog Ollie.